The Witch of Elements

The Witch of Elements

Courtney Kirkpatrick

Published by Courtney Kirkpatrick, 2019.

Title: The Witch of Elements
By: Courtney Kirkpatrick
Copyright © 2019 Courtney Kirkpatrick

Chapter One: The Mysterious Girl

THERE WAS A LEGEND in the village of Moon Shine that promised one day, the world would become dark; some insidious force would take over and block out the light of the world. The Blood Demons were that darkness. Zafira didn't know much about the world of Blood Demons, but the people who did know about them knew them as vicious creatures with horns, fangs as sharp razors, and wings like a dragon's. They were the terrors of the night.

Moon Shine would be the first of many peaceful villages to fall to the horror of the Blood Demons. Moon Shine looked to the moon as their source of life. The moon's bright light was believed to be the source of all light in their village.

However, there was also a legend which foretold of a girl... and once she reached a certain age, she would discover she was no ordinary girl. She would discover she possessed powerful magic that would help her save the world from a horrible fate. If she refused to learn about this incredible magic inside her and didn't accept it, the world as she knew it would fall into a dark pit of despair. Everyone would be enslaved, forced to become blood bags, and would suffer a terrible fate at the hands of the Blood Demons.

It was cold and dark. The snow fell heavily, and the air was chilly. Blood mixed with the pure white snow, turning it a deep crimson red. Zafira ducked down to catch her breath, her brown hair blowing wildly in the wind and her blue eyes frantically searching the skies. Her white cloth shirt, and knee-length brown skirt were both torn. Her legs felt like jelly, her lungs as if they were on fire, and she could feel her body getting ready to collapse and give out.

She knew without a doubt that she had to keep running, though. If she stopped now, they would get her, just like they got her parents and destroyed her village. The Blood Demons were nearby, and she had to escape them or surely, she would be next. She didn't want to die though, she wasn't ready. She wanted to live to see another day.

The winged beasts, better known as the Blood Demons, were roaming the inky black sky above. She had heard in the village just before the attack that they were looking for a 15-year-old girl by the name of Zafira Rose.

Blood Demons were almost like vampires, but with slight differences. Blood Demons had dragon wings that went past their back. Blood Demons also had fangs for teeth like a vampire, and their eyes looked human, but when they were hungry or angry, their eyes were blood red. Blood Demons could also disguise themselves to appear human, unlike vampires. They had spent many years in hiding and were finally ready to take over. They knew of the legend of the Witch of Elements and they were not going to let her survive. They had no idea what she looked like; they only knew she lived in the village known as Moon Shine.

Zafira was more than an ordinary girl she was the key to their destruction. She could destroy them and restore peace. But only if she figured out her true potential.

THE BLOOD DEMONS WERE determined to keep that from happening though, especially the Blood Demon prince. A winged beast by the name of Lucios was searching high and low for the young girl. He was getting frustrated but when all seemed hopeless, he glimpsed at something. He thought he was quietly sneaking up on her, but he had another thing coming. Neither one of them was prepared for the potential she held inside. He didn't know she would lead him to his demise.

ZAFIRA'S LEGS WERE giving out. Her throat felt as if it was catching on fire and her eyes were drooping from exhaustion. She couldn't stop though, she had to keep running. She had no idea what was going on. *Why was she being chased? Why was her village destroyed? Why were they after her? She was just a normal girl, wasn't she?*

Zafira had no idea of her powers, but her parents and village knew. She was supposed to find out about them when she turned sixteen, but she would have to learn about them sooner than that.

Zafira quickly hid behind a tree. She thought back to when her life was simple. Back to when she was happy and when she didn't have to live in fear. Zafira closed her eyes as she pictured the happier time. Back when her parents and the villagers were still alive.

She had a flashback of a memory. *She was about five years old and running around with some of the other kids in her village. She waved to her parents as she played tag with some of the older kids. She couldn't remember their names, she just remembered they were a fun group to play with.*

"Tag! You're it!" she heard a girl say as she tapped Zafira lightly on the shoulder and ran off.

Zafira smiled and laughed in excitement as she went to chase the other kids.

She had always been a happy child. Why couldn't things have remained like that? Why did this tragedy happen? She wished time was still innocent. She wished she could go back and be a happy little girl with no worries. She was so carefree as a child and she wanted that feeling back.

Once she snapped out of her flashback, her legs collapsed, unable to fight the exhaustion her body was experiencing from running. Zafira was in too much pain to move. As she slowly closed her eyes, she saw two pairs of feet coming toward her. That was the last thing she saw before she blacked out.

THE CROWN PRINCE OF the Blood Demons snatched Zafira up in his arms, threw her onto his back, and soared high into the sky. Change was finally going to happen. The Witch of Elements would finally be destroyed. Little did he know, she would be the greatest challenge he would ever face. She would not be destroyed easily.

"Finally, the time has come. The witch will be destroyed, and our kind will reign over the earth," the prince muttered under his breath as he prepared to take flight with his unconscious cargo.

Lucios flew to the kingdom of Red Shadows. Moon Shine was in the east forest and Red Shadows was in the west. Everyone in the village knew the Blood Demons wanted to expand their territory and show everyone the extent of their power. But it was also common knowledge that they could only do that if they destroyed The Witch of Elements. Zafira was the only thing standing in their way.

The sky was red as well as the moon and shadows lurked around every corner. Blood Demons inhabited a village in Red Shadows overlooked by a castle. The castle was run by the royal family who consisted of Lucios and his parents. No other Blood Demons were of royal blood. They were all merely villagers that craved blood. He could hear the thoughts of a few Blood Demons talking below.

She has come!
The time is near!
The Blood Demons will reign soon!
Destruction is near!

The town below was a nightmare. Every demon below had a thirst for blood. Human blood had a sweet and pure taste compared to the blood of an animal. But the blood of the Witch of Elements was what every Blood Demon craved. Rumors had spread that her blood was as sweet as strawberries. Every single Blood Demon in Red Shadows craved her blood and they would fight to the death if that meant getting the chance to taste it. Every Blood Demon wanted to be the first one to try her blood.

Lucios landed in a room with a bed and chains, ignoring the thoughts of his fellow demons. As he laid the young girl down and chained her to the bed, he could not help but admire her beauty. She appeared to be around fifteen years of age. Too young to die, but her fate was already determined by the ancient prophecy. She would be the sacrifice that let his race begin the reign of destruction. Soon, the once peaceful world they lived in would be overrun by the Blood Demons and everyone who lived would either be slaves or blood bags.

He would have killed the girl on the spot while she was unconscious, but he liked to play games. He liked torturing his prey; he wanted to see her suffer and hear her scream. He also wanted to see if she was brave or reckless enough to put up a fight. After all, where was the fun in hunting for food if you couldn't play with it? He wanted to enjoy every moment of torturing the Witch of Elements.

ZAFIRA TOSSED AND TURNED the entire night, the shrieks of her fellow villagers replaying in her mind along with the sound of razor-sharp fangs. The panicked look in her mother's eyes as she told Zafira to run. Dark blood staining the snow. The beat of heavy wings, hidden in the night.

Zafira screamed as she saw her mother and father viciously murdered in front of her eyes. Her body wouldn't move. It wasn't until her mother spoke that she snapped out of her frozen state.

"Zafira, run.... y-you need to s-survive. You are special, you need to run," Sophina said weakly as she looked at her daughter.*

"What do you mean Mother? How am I special? What's going on Mother? Mother!" Zafira cried, but it was too late.*

Sophina gave her daughter a weak smile and collapsed on the floor beside her husband, Ryker, as they took their last breaths together. Zafira wept with her eyes closed as her mother and father died. "No, Mother, Father! Please come back! No, this can't be real!" Zafira sobbed.

It did seem unreal to her, but when Zafira reopened her eyes in her dream, reality sunk in. This was really happening. Her parents and fellow villagers were gone. The Blood Demons had destroyed everyone she loved without remorse. She had no idea what to do. After all, she was only fifteen. What *could* she do?

Zafira looked up from her parents to see the Blood Demons hungrily glaring in her direction as if she were a chunk of meat waiting to be devoured. Her eyes widened and her breathing became heavy. She sprang to her feet and ran from Moon Shine. She was frightened for her life; she didn't want to be the Blood Demons' next meal.

The moon always shined brightly in the village and brought everything to life; that was what had given the village its name, but now everything had been destroyed. Zafira couldn't stay; it was no longer a home, but rather a destroyed, vacant shell of what it once had been. The huts were demolished from the fires and reduced to ash. The crops that once yielded abundant resources were now nothing. All the verdant green plant life in the village had turned to gray ash.

ZAFIRA WOKE WITH A gasp from the horrible dream. At least, she *thought* it had been a dream. However, as she became more aware of her surroundings, she remembered it was indeed real; everything she loved no longer existed. She tried to sit up to clear her head but was pulled back. When she looked down at her hands, she found chains around her wrists.

Tears started to build up in her eyes, but she wasn't going to throw herself a pity party. At least not now. She had to get free before she wallowed in her sadness. She tried yanking on the chains to no avail. No matter how hard she tried, her attempts were futile. She fell back on the bed frustrated, finally releasing her tears and letting her screams escape.

"Help!" Zafira cried. "Someone, please help me!"

Her pleas were ignored....

She was on her own and would have to figure a way out by herself. She was in an unfamiliar place and it frightened her.

Zafira sat helplessly in the dust-filled bed rocking back and forth, her tears falling one after another and plopping down on her lap as she purged her fear and unease, she wanted nothing more than to leave this horrible place. As she sobbed, Zafira couldn't help but notice the shadow flying through the castle window.

"Blood! I crave your blood!" The unknown beast said with his fangs sticking out and his blood-red eyes staring at Zafira with thirst. "I want to see if the rumor is true. I need to see if it tastes sweet as strawberries." What was this beast talking about? Her blood didn't taste like strawberries, did it?

Zafira turned around in fright and screamed as loud as she could with her eyes closed. She heard the Blood Demon's wings lift into the air, which could only mean that he was lunging in for the kill. The Blood Demon went into attack formation, but before he could bite her, an electrical discharge shot from Zafira's hand. The blast sent the Blood Demon right out of the window. After about five minutes, Zafira opened her eyes. She looked around, confused and wondering where the Blood Demon had gone.

She looked down at her hand and saw smoke coming from it. Her hand felt as if it was on fire. She flinched at the burning sensation. *How did that happen?*

Zafira quickly ran to the bed, shivering with fear. She didn't want the Blood Demon to come back and hurt her. She just wanted to go home. She just wanted her parents back.

How did he get out there? Zafira still couldn't wrap her head around what had happened.

The Blood Demon screamed up at her through the window.

"I may have not been able to taste your blood," it shouted, "but you will soon find out what you are here for. It is the end of your existence! Down with the Witch of Elements!"

Witch of Elements? Zafira had heard the legend but didn't think she could possibly be her. She just thought it was old folklore the villagers gossiped about. She even remembered her mother telling her stories about the Witch of Elements. *Was the Witch of Elements really her?*

The attack she had thrown at the Blood Demon must have meant something. Maybe she was a witch. If that was the case, had her parents known? Was that why they, along with her village, had been destroyed? Zafira looked out the window in the dark room. She then noticed a mysterious marking on her right wrist in the shape of a crescent moon beside a sun. She had never seen it before – where had it come from?

Are these the markings of a witch?

Exhausted and overwhelmed, Zafira fell into a deep sleep with tears running down her face, unaware that she would not be so alone when she awoke.

Chapter Two: The Mark

ZAFIRA WAS NEARLY BLINDED by the sun coming through the window. She attempted to stretch, but the chains on her wrists prevented such relief. She sighed in annoyance. The markings were still on her wrists as well.

So, it wasn't a dream.

The door of the room suddenly slammed open, causing her to jump in fright and snap out of her thoughts. A young male strolled into the room. He had long black hair that went down his back, black horns on his head, and eyes that were unusually blue instead of Blood Demon red. She also noticed that he wore a black pendant in the form of a dragon, with red rubies as the eyes and blue jewels along the outer layer of its wings.

"You're up. Perfect," Lucios said in a smooth, chilling voice.

There was something off about him, so Zafira kept her guard up. That proved futile as Lucios sped over to her. This surprised her entirely and caused her entire body to freeze up.

Their bodies were so close that Zafira could hear her heart speeding up in fear. Her heightened emotions made a sly smirk appear on Lucios' face.

"Don't scream or I will personally end your life here and now," Lucios stated.

Trembling, Zafira nodded. She did not want to anger a Blood Demon in fear for her life. Little did she know, no matter what she said or did, he would end her life regardless. He unlocked the chains holding her to the bed and hoisted her onto his back. Before she could utter a single word, he cut her off.

"Hold on tight if you do not wish to fall," Lucios said.

"What do you—"

Before Zafira could finish her sentence, the cold wind blew on her face. She looked around and saw she was high up in the air. This only made her cling to Lucios tighter, fearing that if she let go, she would fall.

AS LUCIOS FLEW THROUGH the midnight sky, he neared his destination: The Chamber of Darkness. This chamber held many dark spells that could destroy any witch and Lucios couldn't wait to use them on Zafira. Soon the Witch of Elements would be no more, and he would take his place as ruler of Moon Shine and any other village he came across. Of course, since his Blood Demon minions had already destroyed Moon Shine, he would just make the town his second castle. He would be better than any other king, simply because he owned two castles instead of one. He would make his parents proud by ruling two kingdoms and showing other creatures that the Blood Demons were in control and they would do well to fall in line.

Lucios' thoughts were interrupted when he saw the chamber in the distance. He sped up, forcing Zafira to shut her watering eyes. He flew into the window of a chamber and roughly shoved her off his back. She landed on the floor with a thud.

"COULD YOU BE A LITTLE gentler?!" Zafira asked under her breath.

The floor that she crash-landed on was cold and damp. The walls around her were gray and mossy. Cracks also filled the walls, and Zafira assumed the place was ancient. There was a wooden table with beakers and test tubes with an unusual color of liquid in them. The walls were lit by flaming torches and had chains hanging on them as well. There was a table in the corner with a myriad of different weapons on it and a black stand with purple scrollwork and an open book.

Lucios clenched his fist. "Watch your mouth, girl!"

"Make me!" Zafira challenged hotly.

She did not know where all this bravery was coming from. It was as if some powerful source of energy had built up within her, just waiting to be unleashed. Normally, she was brave, but she had to be extra careful about what she said or did. If this Blood Demon had killed her parents and her entire village, then there was no telling what else he was capable of.

Before Zafira could even blink, Lucios' hand was firmly around her throat, slowly depleting her oxygen. His speed and strength had taken her by surprise. Zafira grasped his fingers to try and loosen his grip, but the effort was futile.

"Foolish girl! Do you not know who you are speaking to!" Lucios said hatefully. "I am Prince–soon to be King Lucios! I am the son of King Leveron and Queen Marilena, the rulers of Red Shadows!"

"I don't care who you are," Zafira said. "You and those revolting Blood Demons of yours deserve to rot in hell for all the misery you have caused!"

Lucios' blue, ocean-like eyes changed to a virulent blood red as the anger in him grew. He tossed Zafira violently to the ground and then stood above her.

"How dare you challenge my authority?! No one has ever dared to talk back to a Blood Demon! Especially, one of royal blood!" He continued to rant as if she wasn't even in the room.

"You talk tough, but you humans are all the same: weak, pitiful, and pathetic. I do not see how a young girl like you has the ability to destroy us." Lucios glared at the so-called powerful witch.

"What do you mean?" Zafira was confused. "I don't have any abilities. I'm just a normal girl."

He let out an insidious laugh. "You seriously have no idea that you are a witch, do you? Well, destroying you is going to be easier than I thought then."

"What do you mean *destroying* me?" Zafira asked, even though she feared the answer.

"You see, this is a witch chamber, Zafira. You're about to find out exactly what it does to witches like you," he said with a smirk. Her entire body shivered as unease trickled down her spine.

IN LUCIOS' EYES, HE saw what a weak, pathetic, frightened little girl Zafira was. She could not possibly be some type of witch, let alone one who could save the world. Sure, she had a stubborn attitude, like most teenage girls, but he could tell she was frightened by the look in her eyes. He had also noticed the marking on her wrist. It was indeed the mark the Witch of Elements was said to have. The crescent moon and sun represented darkness and light. She really was the Witch of Elements the legend had foretold. He wanted to be an all-powerful king who was feared by many, but he could not do that if this girl stood in his way. It was time for the Witch of Elements to be destroyed, and he would be the one to accomplish the task.

ZAFIRA BACKED AWAY as Lucios began to glow a fiery black. Next thing she knew, a Shadow Blast came right towards her. The markings on her wrist began to glow a light blue and water streamed from her hand, effectively extinguishing the flames. Zafira's eyes widened in amazement. Once the attack had cleared, she stared at her hands in astonishment.

"What was that?" It was true, Zafira realized. She was a witch.

"You wretch! How dare you!" Lucios' eyes boiled with rage as he concentrated on building his power again. He put his hand out and yelled "Dark Chaos!"

Another ball of shadows came hurtling towards her—this one much larger than the last. Zafira stood ready, frozen in place. However, before the conjuring could hit her, water shot from her again. Only this time, the force was too powerful, and it sent her flying into a wall. Smoke filled the room from the blasts.

What was happening to her? What was that? There seemed to be so many secrets hidden inside of her that she had yet to uncover.

When the smoke cleared, Zafira looked up to see Lucios walking towards her. She tried to stand, but her body was in too much pain from the impact. Once he was close enough, Lucios bent down and grabbed her by the shirt, dragging her over to a wall that held more chains. He lifted her hands and wrapped her wrists in the cold metal with which she was becoming all too familiar.

Lucios flipped on a lever that lifted her up off the ground. She tried to struggle and loosen the chains on her wrists, but her attempts were for naught. He laughed as a smirk began to form on his face.

"Struggle all you want. Those are no ordinary chains around your wrists."

Zafira had never really gotten a good look at Lucios until now. His eyes were as blue as the ocean when they were not a fiery red with rage. The red t-shirt he wore highlighted his lean, muscular chest and abs. He wore black pants along with a matching black cape and black boots that shone as dark as the night sky. But she also noticed the sharp fangs in his mouth and his incredibly pale skin. Just the thought of those fangs made Zafira shiver as she imagined those sharp teeth digging into the neck of not only her fellow villagers, but her parents as well.

"Stop staring!" Lucios snapped.

Zafira narrowed her eyes at him. She would not give into temptation. He was an enemy and that was all he would ever be. There was no doubt he was also much older than her. She would not be hypnotized by his good looks. Just because he was handsome did not mean he wasn't her enemy. He would pay for capturing her and killing her loved ones. She just wasn't entirely sure how yet.

"Sorry," Zafira said, gazing at the floor before her.

Lucios grabbed Zafira tightly by the chin forcing her to look straight at his face. She could feel herself getting lost in his eyes. *Snap out of it, Zafira!* She would not get trapped under his hypnotic spell.

"You'd better be, but then again you won't be alive much longer anyway." He grinned.

"W-What do you mean?" No matter how brave Zafira tried to present herself, the fear that Lucios sent down her spine could not be ignored. She was afraid to die. She wanted to live to be older than just fifteen.

Zafira struggled side to side in her restraints, but Lucios merely laughed at her measly efforts. She thought she might have irritated him by fighting back, but it seemed she was doing the complete opposite. He was enjoying this.

"It's useless, girl! Those chains are unbreakable!" Lucios' loud, obnoxious laughter filled the room and she lowered her head dejectedly.

She could feel the tears encroaching. Her parents' murders along with the annihilation of her village, having to run away, being captured, discovering she had powers and some evil demon was trying to destroy her—she knew this wasn't a dream, but she really wished it was. She had to face that this was her reality and not just a dream.

Tears rolled down her cheeks. *Was this how she was going to die? In this cold, dark room, while she was chained up and continuously tortured?* She wanted more out of life. She wanted to go on adventures and explore places she hadn't seen. She wanted to live life to the fullest and be happy. She didn't want to die by the hands of some Blood Demon.

An intense pain suddenly shot through Zafira's body, snapping her out of her morose thoughts.

Lucios then began chanting a spell that caused pain to ricochet throughout her body. *What was happening? Why did her body suddenly feel like it was on fire?* Her insides were starting to burn, and she felt as if all the organs in her body were slowly being burned away one by one. Zafira shut her eyes tightly attempting to escape the pain, but she slowly tried to reopen them only to catch a small glimpse of Lucios' mouth moving.

"Let the fire within burn,
Let it slowly burn the inside,
Make the Witch slowly suffer,
Destroy the Elemental Witch
Let it all end in smoke."

The pain was getting to be too much for her, and she slowly started to drift in and out of consciousness. *What is this? What is he doing to my body?* The agony was so intense that she let out a powerful scream that caused Lucios to chuckle darkly.

Mother, Father, please help me. What do I do? I feel so weak.

"Soon the Witch of Elements will be gone, and I will rule this world unopposed!" Lucios said with another insidious laugh.

Zafira thought she was imagining things, but as she started to close her eyes from exhaustion, she could feel a presence inside of the cold, damp room. But who was it though? The only people in this room were her and Lucios.

"Zafira," came a soft whisper.

The voice sounded like her mother, but how could that be? She had seen her parents murdered in cold blood by Lucios and his fellow Blood Demons. It had to be some sort of spell that he was casting on her, one designed to toy with her emotions.

Zafira opened her eyes a little to see the ghosts of her mother and father. Her eyes widened in shock. She couldn't believe it! Her mother was still beautiful, even as a ghost. She still had her inky black hair, and eyes that were as blue as the springtime sky. Her skin was just pale from being a ghost, but she still radiated in beauty. Her father, Ryker, on the other hand with his dark brown hair, that went past his shoulders and his green eyes still reflected much love for his daughter. He still possessed a slim but muscular physique as well, her mother was still small and dainty as always. Zafira closed her eyes and reopened them, but luckily this wasn't a trick or a dream. They were standing right in front of her.

"Mom, Dad," Zafira said weakly.

"Zafira, my daughter," Ryker said, with his wife standing right next to him with her hand on his bicep.

"Mom, Dad, what am I supposed to do?" Zafira whispered.

Lucios was so absorbed with his spell that he did not notice her lips moving. He could not even see her parents' ghosts—he was completely oblivious to their presence. It was as if only Zafira herself had the ability to see them. But that was impossible? Surely, Lucios could see them, right?

"What do I do, Mom? Dad?" Zafira felt the conflagration within her burning her up from the inside.

"You have the power to escape this, Zafira," her father said.

"H-How though? I feel so weak." She hardly had any energy left in her voice.

"Close your eyes. Breathe in and out slowly, then open your eyes and concentrate," Sophina said with a small smile.

"But how will I know what to do?" Zafira asked worriedly.

"Don't worry. You'll know what to do princess," her father said with confidence. "Goodbye my darling," her mother said with sadness.

"Don't go. Please." She didn't want her parents to leave again.

"We love you, princess," Ryker said with a smile.

Zafira's parents started to disappear, but before they did, they both waved, telling her they loved and believed in her. Zafira snapped out of her conversation with her parents only to let a scream of agony rip loose from her lungs. Her body slowly felt like it was burning from the inside out.

Zafira tried her best to ignore the tears falling down her face. She slowly breathed in and out about three times, before focusing on Lucios and concentrating. Eventually, she could feel a power trickling through her body as she regained her strength. What was happening? Was this her parent's doing? No, this had to be her own strength. She just hadn't been aware she possessed it.

"What are you doing?" Lucios yelled in astonishment.

She could hear his exclamation, but she decided to ignore it. Instead, she concentrated and pulled and yanked on the chains that were binding her to the wall. She yanked as hard as she could until she could hear the metal of the chains begin cracking. After a few more tries, her bonds finally broke. Just before she fell to the floor her body began to shine as brightly as the sun, nearly blinding Lucios.

Once she was free, Zafira glared at Lucios' stupefied expression. She was going to make him pay for making her suffer. She strolled towards her captor, who backed away a bit.

"No! Impossible! Those chains are unbreakable!" Lucios cried.

"Those chains seemed pretty breakable to me," Zafira said with a smirk.

She was scared to use her powers—as she wasn't entirely sure what she was capable of—but, she was determined to use these newfound abilities if they would destroy this monster. The only difference this time was that she was prepared to use them. She didn't care what the drawbacks were; all she cared about was making Lucios pay for nearly burning her alive.

She saw Lucios' eyes turn red with anger, but they also had a tinge of fear hidden within their depths. Zafira heard Lucios scream and his whole body shake with barely concealed rage and power. She quickly saw a stream of energy come out of Lucios' hand and dodged it.

She closed her eyes and threw a ball of electricity right at him, which created the perfect diversion. She seized the opportunity to run as fast as she could away from the chamber. She wanted to destroy Lucios before, but she figured it would be better if she learned more about her powers and how to use them first. If she didn't, there was the possibility of not only destroying Lucios but herself as well.

She ran for what seemed like hours, but it was probably only about forty-five minutes. She could feel the pain in her legs intensifying as she picked up her pace, but she couldn't stop. If she stopped now, the Blood Demons would only find her again and this time she would not be able to escape their clutches.

Zafira ran faster and faster, but a sudden noise in the forest made her jump. Straightening her posture, she knew she had to be brave and stay strong. She had to avenge her parents and village. She couldn't let a little noise in the forest dissuade her from her goals.

She looked back to see if he was still following her, or if he had summoned backup, sighing in relief when she didn't spot a single Blood Demon. She was safe for now. A light shown through the trees and she continued to run, even though her lungs were screaming for oxygen, Zafira hoped the light would lead her somewhere safe. She couldn't let the pain she felt—not only in her body, but her heart–stop her from escaping.

Once she reached the trees, Zafira scanned the area. It was strange to her that this village did not just have one type of creature, but she saw fairies, vampires, pixies, and many more drift past her as she gazed at this unusual village. *How is that possible though?* Most of the villages that she had known had only ever had one kind of species in each village. Well, by "species" she meant "humans". So, what made this village different? Why were there all these different types of demons living together?

All these other creatures were not human, but demons of different species. No one was the same, she saw demons with horns, claws, wings, and some that had scaly features and some of them even looked almost human-like. She may have heard the villagers, or perhaps her parents talk about demons before, but she never believed they existed. The villagers had said that demons were creatures that weren't necessarily human and had powerful demonic abilities.

Zafira cautiously left the safety of the trees and proceeded to walk towards the village. The creatures looked at her curiously. All the demons in the village were staring at her, whispering to each other, and pointing at her. She didn't know if it was because she was human or if it was because she looked horrible from being tortured. She scanned the crowds for any humans, but all she saw were mythical creatures. At least she thought they were mythical, but then again, she supposed if Blood Demons were possible, then any type of demon was possible.

Zafira's eyes widened when she saw what appeared to be some type of demon coming towards her. She knew she shouldn't judge, but she couldn't trust anyone.

"There's no need to be frightened. My name is Maya Tallulah. I'm a wolf demon. What are you?" Maya asked.

Zafira took a good look at Maya and noticed she had black hair pulled back in a high ponytail and nature-like green eyes. She wore black armor with red accents. Her armor also consisted of brown wolf fur. She appeared to be about seventeen years old. Even though she claimed to be a wolf demon, she didn't come off as terrifying.

"M-My name is Zafira. I'm h-human," Zafira struggled to answer.

"I could smell it on you. You look like you have been through a lot," she could hear the worry in Maya's voice.

"I have," Zafira agreed sadly.

"Well let's get you cleaned up," Maya said and helped Zafira to her feet.

As Maya led her to one of the many little huts in the village, she studied what looked like other wolf demons like Maya, who likewise stared back. She cast her eyes away and dutifully followed Maya. Maya helped Zafira lie down while she went to get some warm water, bandages, and some healing medicine.

Maya got right to the point when she had come back with her supplies. "So, what happened to you?"

Zafira took off her shirt and skirt, which really was more of a rag now, ruined from running through the forest and battling the Blood Demons. Maya started to rub the medicine onto her bruises and abrasions. She winced as the medicine contacted the tender skin of her stomach, but she would survive the pain. It was nowhere near as bad as when Lucios was trying to burn her. Zafira noticed that Maya seemed to be quite skilled in medicine and treating injuries. The pain was bearable thanks to Maya's help.

"It's a long story." She sighed and said, as Maya bandaged her wounds.

"I have time."

"How do you know so much about medicine?" Zafira asked before they got into what happened to her.

"My mother had healing abilities and knew a lot about medicine and taught me everything," Maya said. "Now spill, what happened to you?"

"About two or three nights ago—I can't remember how long it was, time seems to have blended together—but my village was destroyed. A group of Blood Demons slaughtered everyone in my village. I managed to escape alive, but the prince captured me and brought me to his kingdom and tortured me. It may sound crazy, but my parents...well, their spirits told me that I had what it took to free myself. I felt this immense power rise up in me and the next thing I knew I had broken free from my chains and I was running for my life and ended up here." Zafira could still not wrap her head around the idea of being a witch.

"Wow. That's quite an adventure," Maya said as she finished up her ministrations and gathered up her supplies.

"I know, but now I have to figure out how to control my powers," Zafira said sadly while her body shook in sadness.

"I think I know someone who could help."

"Really?!" Zafira brightened. "That would be wonderful!"

"Wait here." Maya left the room.

Zafira sighed and lay down, slowly closing her eyes. She didn't mean to fall asleep, but once she was, she dreamed of her parents.

"Zafira, love, you have to wake up," she could hear her mother say.

"Mom? Is that you?" Zafira glanced around what appeared to be some type of forest.

"Yes dear, it is me," her mother's voice confirmed. *"Zafira, you must train with Raidon. He can help you control your powers."*

"But how do I find him, Mother?" Zafira asked.

"You are where he lives. Your new friend Maya will help you, but first, my daughter you must awake!"

Zafira came to, gasping for air. Zafira looked up as she heard someone come into the hut. She saw Maya and what appeared to be some sort of demon. He had long brown hair all the way to his back and red eyes that looked as if they were encapsulated by fire themselves. He had a muscular build, and he wore black pants and a black robe slightly flared open with a flame design on the outline of his robe that showed off his chest. To Zafira, he put off a dangerous vibe. He also had black wings, but unlike the dragon-like wings of the Blood Demons, these were feathery—almost like a fairy or angel's wings. She thought the wings that he held seemed unusual; almost unreal. She was shocked that this creature possessed such features. His black boots made a clunking sound every time he took a step.

Her eyes widened in fear. He might not be a Blood Demon, but Zafira did not like any demon. They frightened her, and she did not know whether the man standing next to Maya could be trusted. Of course, Maya was a demon and she had trusted her right away, but she gave off a friendly persona. This demon gave Zafira the chills for some reason. She was going to do her best to stand her ground and stay on his good side. That's if he even had one.

Maya walked over to Zafira and bent down in front of her with a soft smile.

"Zafira, it is okay. This is Raidon. He can help you learn to control your powers." Maya offered her a hand up off the ground.

Zafira didn't know if she should take Maya's hand to meet this demon named Raidon or not. Her mother said he was supposed to help her with her powers, but could she really trust him? Maya did, so maybe she should give him a chance. Zafira sighed as she took Maya's hand, making her first attempt at standing her ground around this Raidon character.

Raidon studied Zafira's behavior. "Is this the girl?"

"Yes. She is the one." Maya's voice snapped Zafira out of her musings.

"She looks weak. She would give up by the end of the day," Raidon said, staring at Zafira with a stern expression. *What is with everyone calling her weak! It was getting to be annoying!* She was not weak; she just didn't know how to control these so-called powers.

"Give her a chance," Maya reasoned. "She could surprise you, Raidon." At least she had confidence in her newfound friend's abilities.

While they talked back and forth, Zafira did not know what to do. She did feel weak, but she wanted to prove to this demon here that she was not. Before she knew what she was doing, she was walking up to Raidon and getting into his face, ignoring the pain she was in to speak her thoughts aloud.

"I AM SICK AND TIRED of everyone calling me weak!" She blurted out angrily. "I am *not* weak! I just don't know how to control these goddamn powers! So how about you just shut that smart mouth of yours and teach me how to control them!"

Raidon laughed.

"What is so funny?" Zafira yelled in frustration.

How dare he laugh at her! He didn't even know her!

"I was waiting for you to say something," Raidon answered with a haughty sneer. "I knew if I riled you up it would prove that you were worthy of my training."

"What is wrong with you?" She could not believe this guy's twisted sense of humor. "Are you sick in the head?"

"No, I'm just easily entertained." Raidon laughed again.

"Just ignore him," Maya said. "I do. He doesn't have the best sense of humor in the world."

"I do too! Anyway, onto more important matters. Your training will be intense. Do you think you can handle it?" Raidon asked with an arched eyebrow.

"Yes." There was an ounce of doubt in her tone. This demon seemed to be childish. Could he really have the power necessary to train her?

"Are you sure?" Raidon fixed her with a stern gaze. It felt like he could see right through her. It was as though he could see right in her very soul, straight to that kernel of doubt she held deep down.

"Yes, I am sure." Zafira was confident now. "But are you sure you can train me? I mean your little stunt to get me riled up was extremely childish."

"While I only appear to be eighteen in human years, technically I'm one-hundred and eighty in demon years." Raidon clarified. "I may not seem like it, but I like to get people worked up. I've got to get my entertainment where I can."

"That is messed up. But I am ready to train with you." Zafira said with steely determination in her voice.

"Very well. Your training will begin tomorrow. Until then, get some rest. You will need it. Meet me in the middle of the forest east of here when the sun begins to rise. Maya will make sure you are ready." Raidon then left, acknowledging Maya with a nod, but stopped abruptly. "And to know you are in the right location, you will see some trees with burn marks and scratches on them." Raidon then continued on his way.

Chapter Three: Training

IT WAS NOT LONG BEFORE the sun was starting to peek its rays over the horizon. Zafira had gotten little sleep by the time Maya was waking her up. Maya had made an outfit out of wolf hide for Zafira to wear while training—a top from white fur and the skirt black; the armor was made of fangs and claws. Once she was dressed, Maya led her over to the trees where Raidon said they would meet. Once they showed up in the middle of the forest east of the village, she looked around to see if she was in the right location. She saw burn marks and some trees scratched up. She assumed that she was indeed in the right location.

"Where is he?" Zafira asked, looking around; she could not see Raidon anywhere. She had no time to play games.

"He will be here," Maya said with a smile. "Do not worry."

Zafira waited for a good thirty minutes, growing impatient until Raidon decided to show his face. He was wearing black pants, with a simple white top, and some black boots, he was pulling on some black fingerless gloves with a flame design on the sides as he approached them.

"Finally!" She exclaimed impatiently. "Where were you?"

"Not that it is any of your concern, but I had to feed before I trained you," Raidon replied. "Now shall we begin?"

Zafira stiffened. *Feed?* Feed on what? Was he like the Blood Demons or was he some other kind? She shook her head and tried to clear her thoughts. No. She couldn't think about that. At least not right now. She had to concentrate if she wanted to get stronger.

"Yes. Where shall we begin?" Zafira answered.

"First, we will focus your energy," Raidon said. "If you do not do this, your powers will be harder to control."

"Okay. So how do I focus my energy?"

"Close your eyes, focus your thoughts, and strike. You should feel a source of energy running through your body." Raidon instructed.

As Zafira concentrated, she could hear Raidon's footsteps circling her. It was as if he was testing her to see if she was really concentrating. Little did she know it was something completely different.

Eyes closed, Zafira was completely unaware of what was happening until Maya shouted,

"Zafira, look out!"

Zafira spun around, dodging Raidon's punch from behind. Raidon glared at Maya and she shied away.

"Stay out of this," he barked. "This is part of her training." Raidon turned his attention back to Zafira.

He lunged at Zafira again, but she anticipated it and he missed. She slowly tried to pull her concentration together and suddenly she felt her hand begin to burn. She looked down in shock and spotted her hand glowing red. She quickly pushed her hand out hoping an attack would hit Raidon, but nothing but a small spark comes out. Zafira then closed her eyes and took a deep breath and reopened her eyes. The mark around Zafira's wrist began to glow a shade of light blue. She felt her hand becoming wet with water. *How is this happening? Why is my hand filling with water? There's barely any water around, except the wet ground.* Zafira snapped out of her thoughts as she was nearly thrown to the floor. She tried throwing a water attack yet, it was weak once again. Raidon, flipped into the air, avoiding her attempt as if it was nothing. This only served to frustrate her more.

"That was good, but not good enough!" Electricity emanated from his hands, shooting towards her. The electricity moved quickly, arcing almost invisibly toward her. She barely had any time to react as the powerful galvanism attack met her body. Zafira let out a powerful scream as the conjure met with her body.

"Thunder Serpent." Zafira heard Raidon shout as the electricity continued to shock her body. The impact of the blitz caused Zafira to go flying into a tree; she slid to the ground trying to catch her breath.

"What was that?" Zafira said.

"My conjure, known as Thunder Serpent. Each type of magical creature has magical abilities that they can draw power from. When we either think or announce the name of our conjure, we have the ability to control how powerful we want that technique to be." Raidon quickly explained and then hurled another Thunder Serpent in Zafira's direction.

She rolled quickly out of the way, getting back to her feet. This was going to be harder than she thought; Raidon was a tough opponent.

"Get up! Is that the best you can do? This is no time to be weak!" Raidon yelled.

Anger boiled within her. She was *not* weak! She couldn't be, right? She would prove it no matter how much training she had to go through. Zafira stood her ground.

"I am not weak!" Zafira yelled in anger.

"Then prove it to me!" Raidon ordered, advancing again, but she quickly spun out of his reach. Slamming the ground, it began to shake under their feet. She launched into the air and threw a sphere of water which mixed with Raidon's leftover electricity. This maneuver was a little bit more powerful than the last. Perhaps because Raidon needled her and made her ire flare up? Raidon was unable to dodge both attacks, and he slammed against a tree, causing him to groan and spit out a bit of blood. However, as soon as she hit the tree Raidon's body engulfed in flames and disappeared.

Zafira landed, keeping her guard up. She did not see Raidon anywhere, but it could be just a test to make sure she was on full alert. She looked up through the trees and around the rocks, but she could not see him. Just then, she sensed something behind her. Spinning around, she was met with a bolt of electricity coming from Raidon's hand.

"Lightning Quake!" Raidon proclaimed

Zafira slid far across the training field and up against a tree once again. She groaned as her back collided with the rough bark. How had he snuck up on her like that? She didn't even see him or better yet hear him approaching until it was too late.

"I'll admit that was good, but not good enough!" Raidon called. "You must be prepared to face an attack from any direction. If you are not prepared, it will be your downfall." Raidon yelled in anger.

"What else do you expect me to do!" Zafira yelled back at him as soon as she had recovered from his previous blow.

"Concentrate and focus!" He growled. "Then you will know what to do!" There was a flare of determination in his eyes.

"How can I concentrate with you attacking me?!" Zafira cried.

"Just try!" Raidon insisted.

Zafira closed her eyes again as she had before, trying to concentrate. Slowly, she focused her energy. Raidon went to attack her once more, her mark then started to glow red, and time seemed to slow down. Once she opened her eyes, she threw a powerful conjure of fire directly at Raidon. It was so powerful he sailed about five hundred feet into the forest. Zafira looked down at her hands that were still glowing in shock. Why were her hands glowing? Did the glowing mean that the conjuring was finally working right?

Raidon appeared to be in shock for a moment but shook it off and appeared right in front of Zafira. Had that not phased him? It was as if the conjure hadn't made any type of impact.

"Raidon is a demon, and unlike humans, demons can withstand more pain. We also have the capability of healing faster than humans." Maya explained clearing up Zafira's confused thoughts.

"That is what I mean," Raidon said. "You have finally learned about your mark and the power that it gives you. Now you must learn to control it. If you do not, it could be dangerous to not only yourself but others as well." He shot a fire conjure at Zafira, yet this one was different. The fire wasn't yellow, orange and red like most fire. This fire was black and dark almost like a shadow.

"Flames of Shadow." Zafira could hear Raidon shout.

She evaded the flames, but this technique was different. It did not blow up, but rather continued to follow her. Her eyes widened in shock and she quickly dodged again. However, the dark fire would not be destroyed. What was this conjure? Why did it keep stalking her? Just exactly what type of demon was this guy anyway?

"If you want the attack to stop," Raidon said, "you must find a way to destroy it yourself!"

Zafira ducked as the ball of black flames missed and flew over her head. Taking a defensive stance, she got ready to face the attack head-on. She focused her thoughts and her hands started to glow a blinding yellow. A bright beam of light then collided with the black fiery shadow. When the two conjures collided, an explosion occurred. As the smoke cleared, Zafira saw Raidon standing in the same position with a few scratches; it was as if her efforts barely fazed him. *What would I have to do to faze him?* Nothing she threw was working.

"That was good, but you have a lot more to learn about your powers," Raidon said with a stern, yet calm tone as he dusted himself off. "We will stop today, but this is only the beginning of your training. You should rest. It is only going to get harder from here on out."

Raidon finished straightening his clothing. Then without a word, he disappeared in a gust of flames, leaving Zafira standing there with her mouth agape.

"He always does that," she explained. "It's nothing new, really. Now, let's get you cleaned up. Training with Raidon will not be easy now that he's seen what you can do." There was a hint of concern in Maya's voice.

"I can take whatever he throws at me. I'll prove to him I am not weak."

As Zafira and Maya entered the hut, thoughts of Raidon still lingered in her head. Was he a fire demon? A shadow demon? He had multiple powers, but none like hers. He could control some elements, but not all. She watched Maya as she got ready for bed and wondered if she should ask her. But would that be out of line?

"Hey, Maya?" Zafira asked.

"Yeah?" Maya smoothed the bedding onto the mattress.

"Can I ask you something?" Zafira doubted she would get an actual answer out of her.

"Sure. What is it?" Maya smiled.

"What kind of demon is Raidon? I mean, he has many different powers. I was just wondering if you knew..." The curiosity was killing her.

"Oh, Raidon? He's a half-demon," Maya answered simply.

"A half-demon? What's that?"

"Well, Raidon was born with two different types of parents." Her smile became sad. "Each of his parents was a different form of demon."

"But I thought there were just full demons?" Zafira said, still confused.

"No, that's not true. In fact, we have quite a few half-demons in our village. We have some that are part human, but there are not many of the human parents left. Half-demons born of a human parent are often difficult pregnancies. Most of the time, if the mother is not strong enough, she dies in childbirth. However, we have had some instances where the mother has survived the birth with just some cracked ribs. When two demons birth a child though, that is a different story. The mother almost always survives since their bodies are built differently from a human. Anyway, Raidon is what we call a half-demon. He doesn't like to talk about it, so don't ask him—and don't tell him that I told you." Maya's expression turned serious.

"Okay, I won't, but what type of demon exactly is Raidon. I mean I know he's a half-demon now, but what type? Like what type of demons were his parents?" Zafira asked.

"Well, believe it or not, his father was a vampire," Maya said. "And Raidon's mother was an elemental fairy," Maya said

"How is a vampire different from a Blood Demon?" Zafira asked Maya with confusion clearly written on her face.

"Unlike the Blood Demons, vampires cannot change their form to appear human. Their eye color cannot change and unlike Blood Demons, their wings are slightly different. Also, unlike Blood Demons who feed primarily on humans and occasionally animals, vampires can choose to feed on animals, blood bags or humans. Blood Demons are also a lot harder to kill than a vampire. But the main thing is their wings. Vampire wings tend to be a lot thinner and slightly smaller than those of a Blood Demon—who has dragon wings that come past their back. But those are only a few differences."

"Wow," Zafira said unable to believe it.

"Yeah, it's not your typical pairing, but then again, no one in this village really is. The only difference really between you and Raidon's mother is that elemental fairies can control only so many elements—like three or four, I believe. I'm not sure about the exact amount, but it's less than you are able to control."

"Oh wow. I had no idea." Zafira said now understanding Raidon and his conjures a little better.

"Yeah, well like I said, it's not something he likes to talk about so don't mention it. He lost his parents when he was about your age, maybe younger. I'm not sure how, but it's painful for him to remember. Now let's get some sleep or Raidon will kill me for keeping you up late." Yawning, Maya laid down to sleep.

Zafira slowly followed Maya and crawled into bed herself. She was happy to know a bit more about not only Raidon but demons in general. It must not have been easy for Maya to tell her knowing she could possibly get in trouble, but Zafira was glad that Maya trusted her enough to open up.

Chapter Four: I Am Not Weak!

ZAFIRA TRIED TO CATCH her breath as the fierce training with Raidon continued. It had been five days since she started her training and she felt stronger than ever, but Raidon said she still needed to work on her powers. She knew that was true, but she needed a rest.

"Can we take a break?" Zafira panted.

"Do you think the Blood Demons will let you take a break?" Raidon said annoyed.

Before Zafira could answer, Raidon flung his Flare Blitz at her. She quickly evaded his attack and hurled a counterattack of water.

"Hydro Beam!"

He avoided the assault as if it was nothing and laughed. He *laughed!* Was this funny to him?

"That barely hurt. You are weak!" Raidon chuckled.

Anger filled Zafira. Every insult that he had hurled at her made her blood boil. His insults were making her angrier and angrier by the minute. The fact that he continued to throw insults at her only made her want to attack him head-on. She did not know how many times she had to say it to get it through his thick skull, but she was not weak. She would prove it.

"I am not weak!" Zafira bellowed, shooting a powerful water conjure at Raidon.

Raidon flipped in mid-air as if he'd been expecting it. She couldn't believe him; he just yawned sarcastically. Zafira looked at Raidon and could tell that he wasn't even breaking a sweat. Zafira was giving her all, but he seemed like he wasn't even out of breath.

"Prove it then!" Raidon yelled, throwing a shadow conjuring with flames flickering around it in Zafira's direction.

"Shadow Fire!" She heard Raidon exclaim.

Zafira's eyes widened, but at the last second, she moved out of the way. She then turned to face the flames, electing to send a blast of water with a dose of electricity straight into the heart of the flames. The impact caused the ground to shake under their feet, but she planted her feet and stood strong against the onslaught.

"Where are you?" She said to herself, scanning the area for Raidon; he had managed to disappear again. He seemed to be doing that a lot lately.

Zafira closed her eyes and focused. She could hear rustling in the trees, so she shot sparks of lightning in that direction in hopes of hitting Raidon.

Lightning Blade. Zafira thought.

All movement stopped for a few moments but was then followed by a burst of fire heading towards her from behind. Zafira jumped just as the fiery assault neared her. She lowered herself enough to sweep Raidon to the floor and threw a conjure of fire that looked like a flower called Fire Bloom at him.

"I told you I am not weak!" Zafira repeated, glaring down at Raidon. "I will prove to you and those Blood Demons that I have what it takes to defeat them." She spoke as if she was trying to reassure herself, more than she was Raidon. She wanted to believe she was not weak. She wanted to prove everyone wrong, even herself.

"Could have fooled me!" Raidon grabbed her by the arm and tossed her over his shoulder.

Zafira flipped in the air and slid to catch herself from hitting a tree. She was getting tired of always hitting the trees because of Raidon. Zafira then slammed the field with her fist, causing a boulder to head straight for Raidon.

Gaia Wave. Zafira thought as she watched the boulder almost hit Raidon.

He managed to dodge the boulder, but he did not see Zafira creeping stealthily up behind him. Raidon gasped in surprise, unable to get out of the way.

Zafira threw a burning orb mixed with electricity right at Raidon. It hit him before he could defend himself.

"Fiery Current!"

"Am I weak *now*?" Zafira asked as Raidon struggled to stand.

Raidon was too proud to admit defeat. He just got up slowly and wiped the blood away from his lip with a smug look on his face.

"Is that the best you can do? You are still just a frail, defenseless little girl!"

Raidon ran at Zafira, kicking and punching. Zafira was barely able to block all the blows and got hit a few times, but it wasn't anything that she couldn't handle. Zafira would admit that even though Raidon was a half-demon, he was no ordinary half-demon. He was fast and barely made it possible for her to keep up with his shadow like attacks.

EVEN THOUGH HE KNEW how to get her blood boiling, she was impressed with his different elemental conjuring's and his speed.

Zafira managed to block most of them, but some were too fast even for her. She got hit a few times, but that did not stop her. Ducking, she conjured an attack mixed with all the elements she could think of—water, fire, earth, air, and electricity—and threw the beam right at Raidon.

"Elemental Fate!"

This conjure was different from the others. All the elements she could think of mixed into one and turned into a huge water beam filled with steam from all the other elements being conjoined with it. Not only did this attack knock Raidon out, but as soon as the technique she threw was over Zafira fell to her knees.

"I am not weak. I am not weak. I am not weak!" Zafira muttered to herself as she grasped the dirt beneath her fingers. She was satisfied with her training for today and didn't think that she could handle anymore. Zafira could feel tears filling her eyes as she grasped the dirt tighter and tighter.

"I'll prove Raidon wrong!" She screamed through her tears. "I'll prove those Blood Demons wrong! I'll prove Lucios wrong!"

Her body hurt all over, but once she was recovered, she would train some more. She would do whatever it takes to defeat those Blood Demons and if she had to train longer and harder, she would. She did not know what was happening, but it was as if all the anger she felt inside had unleashed this hidden power. Suddenly, she felt stronger and was able to stand. The power made her believe that nothing could stop her from defeating Lucios and learning to harness the deep powers hidden inside of her.

The power of all the elements that she learned she could control, made her feel determined. She had no idea that she could control elements such as fire, water, and electricity just to name a few. The power that was lying dormant in her was far from being discovered. She had only unearthed a small portion of her power. There was much more she had yet to discover. Along, with a renewed sense of determination, she felt braver and was no longer scared about what was happening to her. With the help of Raidon and Maya, she was sure to understand her powers more.

Chapter Five: The Hidden Powers

ZAFIRA DID NOT SLEEP that night, too many thoughts running unchecked through her head. She pushed herself to figure out what this new hidden power was inside of her. Zafira wondered how she could figure out how to control these new powers.

Giving up on sleep, she climbed out of bed and headed into the forest near the village. She needed to let her anger out, so she decided to train to see if she could learn anything new. She closed her eyes and breathed deep and drew her focus inward. A strong energy force began to flow through her. The energy felt like her body was slightly burning, but the sensation was not unbearable. Zafira then opened her eyes and her hands were glowing red as she threw a ball of fire at a tree. The blast made a small scorch mark on the bark, but not enough to destroy it. She groaned in frustration. Once again, she closed her eyes. Maybe, if she focused more, the conjure would be stronger?

Focus!

She took a deep breath and then exhaled.

Eternal Scorch. Zafira thought as the fire headed for the tree.

This time when she blasted the tree, it made a bigger mark, yet the tree still stood. She got even more frustrated and continued to throw blast after blast.

She almost fell to the ground in exhaustion and defeat; there had to be a way for her to control her powers so that she did not tire so easily.

"*Zafira.*" She heard a whisper in the wind.

"Mother?" Zafira said, looking around. She saw nothing and sighed in disappointment. Maybe she had imagined it.

"*Zafira,*" She heard her mother's voice float in the wind again, "*don't give up. You can control your powers. You can defeat Lucios. You must believe in yourself. Believe in yourself, just like your father and I believe in you.*"

"*Your mother is right,*" Her father's voice whispered through the trees. "*Believe in yourself my daughter and you will be able to defeat Lucios and bring the light back to our world.*"

Just like that, her parents were gone once again. *Why did they have to die? Why! This is all Lucios' fault. He will pay!* Standing, Zafira blasted fire, the electricity, and then earth magic at a tree nearby.

IT FELL TO THE GROUND in flames. As the fire crackled, Zafira was satisfied, yet she knew she had to continue. She had to become stronger. Tears running down her face, she trained even harder with the knowledge of what happened to her parents sitting at the forefront of her mind. They hadn't deserved to die; they should have still been here with her.

Zafira did what her parents told her. She started to believe in herself and in her powers. She would do this. No. She *could* do this. She could defeat Lucios. She just had to keep reassuring herself that everything would turn out for the better in the end. That, and she also had to believe in herself and not let her self-doubt overpower her.

Zafira practiced every element that she could think of: earth, water, fire, lightning attacks and more. Each time she practiced, the more powerful the various conjures became. As she began to master her elemental powers, she started to discover different combinations. This only made her practice more, wanting to improve in any way she could. She was proud of herself.

She could make a tornado out of fire, which she called Tornado Flare, she was able to throw combinations of different elements in Elemental Combo, and she could even put herself into the attack without damaging her body called Elemental Protection. No move was alike, each came with its own unique capabilities.

Once the sun began to rise, she fell to her knees. She was exhausted, but content. She promised herself before she fell to the ground, that she would defeat Lucios if it was the last thing she'd do. She just had to become stronger and make her parents proud. With the progress she had made in one night, she knew she was on the right track. Zafira then collapsed and fell asleep.

Chapter Six: Strong

ZAFIRA WOKE UP TO THE sun blinding her. *What happened?* She groaned at the myriad of aches and pains in her body. After her eyes had adjusted, she saw Raidon standing above her. She then remembered the intense training she had put herself through and was dreading more.

"About time you woke up," He said. "We have wasted enough time. Get up, go eat something, and we will continue your training." Raidon then jumped up into the trees—most likely to hunt to get his strength up; from what it seemed like Raidon either enjoyed human food or he went off to feed on animals. He didn't seem like the type of person to feed off humans, even though his father was a vampire. He'd been knocked out for a while. No wonder he was hungry. Zafira smiled at the thought of knocking Raidon unconscious again.

She headed back to the hut where she knew she would find Maya. Once Maya saw her, she rushed to Zafira's side to help with her injuries. Once she cleaned Zafira up, she brought her some food. Zafira didn't know what the food was, but she was so hungry that she didn't particularly care. She just dug right in and inhaled the food as if it was nothing. Finished, she stood up and stretched her sore muscles and then headed out to train once more. She needed all the practice she could get if she was to defeat Lucios.

Once she arrived at the place where she and Raidon trained she stood and waited for him to come back. Zafira looked around the clearing assessing the damage she had created while practicing. A few of the trees had ash on them from her fire attacks. Some of the other trees had fallen over from her other elemental powers. Zafira felt proud of herself knowing that she had improved in her abilities a little bit.

She closed her eyes and concentrated and stood with her guard up. She had learned that Raidon waited for her to have her defenses down before he attacked. She was not going to give him the satisfaction this time. She was going to show him she'd improved. She was not weak; all that training she did last night wasn't for nothing.

It was almost too quiet. Suddenly, she felt a chill in the wind. Zafira quickly felt her hand heat up, she looked at her hand to see a fireball had built up in her hand. Not having enough time to overthink things. Spinning around, Zafira opened her eyes and threw a fiery assault.

"Eternal Scorch!" She proclaimed right as Raidon tried to strike. Her fire blasted him against a tree, causing Raidon to hit the tree hard.

A groan escaped Raidon's mouth. "Your strike was stronger than before. I'm impressed."

"I've had some time to practice while you were knocked out," Zafira said with a smirk.

Raidon ignored her newfound optimism. "We'll see how much that practice has paid off then."

"I'll show you." Zafira concentrated.

She blocked any distracting thoughts out of her mind. All she cared about was proving to Raidon that she had improved. She took a deep breath and released, she instantly felt calmer. Her full concentration would now solely be on fighting Raidon.

An immense power ran through her as she threw the move, she had decided to call Eternal Scorch at him, but he dodged it right at the last minute. She frowned in frustration. She would not let her frustration show through. If she allowed it to take over and show, then she would lose control. She had to remain calm and focused if she wanted to prove to Raidon that she was stronger than before.

Just concentrate. She told herself.

Zafira then closed her eyes once more and breathed in and out. The power she felt thrumming throughout her body was incredible. The burning in her body had intensified, which made Zafira clench her teeth in pain, but she would bear it if this new technique she was going to try would work. Her energy felt as if it increased significantly, compared to how it was before. She almost felt; no she did feel much stronger. She opened her eyes and threw a fire sphere mixed with lightning that was speeding right towards Raidon, the conjuring was practically impossible to dodge.

"Fiery Current," Zafira spoke in a whisper.

The blast hit Raidon head-on causing him to crash through some trees. The attack she had thrown would have killed a human, but seeing as Raidon was a half-demon, he only sustained a few injuries.

"Who's weak now?" Zafira said with a grin.

"I will not be made a fool of!" Raidon yelled as he recovered and flew right for Zafira, who easily dodged his counterattack.

She threw Fiery Current at Raidon, but he easily evaded the fire. Slamming her hands into the ground, she caused the earth beneath them to shake.

Gaia Shake. Thought Zafira as she watched Raidon lose his footing and stumble slightly.

Zafira kept her balance, but Raidon was not so lucky. This gave her the opportunity to strike, and she raced so fast that she was almost invisible when she hit Raidon with a lightning bolt made of fire.

Fire Bolt.

The impact caused Raidon to slide and hit a tree.

Zafira threw another Lightning Flame before Raidon had the chance to get up. The blast hit Raidon striking him in the gut. He looked up at Zafira as he slowly regained his footing.

"I will fight Lucios and I will win!" Zafira announced. "I will win this land's freedom and I will avenge my village; I will avenge my parents and everyone else he has caused misery!"

Whirling around, she threw Eternal Scorch one more time at Raidon. The blast had once more knocked Raidon out of the way and caused his body to skid across the dirt on the forest floor. He wiped his mouth with the back of his hand and looked at this girl with a stern look.

"I will say that I am impressed," He said as he stood on his wobbly knees. "You seem ready enough to face the dark road ahead of you."

She was surprised by Raidon's compliment, but she appreciated it, nonetheless. She was glad that she had improved enough with her abilities to impress Raidon.

A fiery passion burned in her eyes as she looked at Raidon and felt the strength inside her continue to grow. She was ready. She was ready to face the demons that had destroyed her family. She was ready to hunt Lucios and his Blood Demons down and destroy him. She was no longer afraid of him.

She was confident and felt as if she had a strong power inside of her that would finally defeat the monsters who tormented her world.

Chapter Seven: The Journey

ZAFIRA WAS GOING TO finally face her fears—come face to face with Lucios.

Lucios.

The name felt like acid on her tongue as she thought about that monster. It sounded like the name of a snake. While he may not physically have been a snake, that's how she saw him. He was sneaky, cruel, and untrustworthy and Zafira just loathed him. He was not going to get away with the destruction and despair he had caused. He needed to pay for his sins, and she was going to make sure that he did. She was going to make him burn.

"Zafira," Maya said concern clear in her voice.

"What is it?" Zafira asked, anxious to leave as well as concerned for the worried expression on her friend's face.

"You can't go alone." Maya finally said, her voice shaking.

"I have to go. I have to avenge my parents' death!" Fury raged through Zafira; she would not be stopped.

"But does that mean you have to go alone?" Maya asked.

"What are you saying?" Zafira was confused.

"I'm saying I'm going with you," Maya said and grabbed her armor and put it on. Zafira watched as Maya slipped on her chest protector over the shirt she was wearing and then slipped on her belt.

"What's the belt for?" Curiosity finally getting the best of Zafira.

"It has some medicines and herbs in case I have to heal anyone," Maya replied.

Once Maya was done getting her armor on Zafira saw her go over to a wooden chest in the corner of the hut. *What was she doing? We need to get going now!* Zafira thought impatiently as she saw her friend open the chest. She could see Maya grabbing something from the chest but couldn't tell what it was. Once Maya turned around, Zafira saw some type of cloth in her hand but couldn't tell what it was since it was folded. As soon as Maya walked over to Zafira, she stood in front of her and held out the cloth-like material for her to take. Zafira took the soft fabric from her friend and unfolded it to see a green dress with a yellow v shape outlining on the waist, sleeves, and the bottom of her dress. The dress also had her mark which was a crescent-shaped moon beside a sun in white with blue outlining around the sun and moon.

Zafira stared in amazement at the dress. She couldn't believe that Maya had gone through so much trouble to make this. She really didn't have to do such a thing. She would surely have to repay her somehow for her kindness.

"Maya I can't accept this. It's too much," Zafira started to argue, "I can just wear one of your outfits."

Maya waved her hand nonchalantly, effectively cutting Zafira's protest off.

"Nonsense, this dress will bring you luck, I had it infused with healing magic," Zafira had a hard time accepting that someone she had known for only a short amount of time cared enough to try and protect her. She truly did not know what she would have done these past few weeks without Maya. She honestly didn't want Maya to go. She did not want to put her friend in harm's way, and she couldn't bear the thought of losing another person she cared about to the Blood Demons. It just didn't sit well with Zafira. But she had a feeling that if she tried to talk Maya out of going, she really wouldn't get far.

"Are you sure? I mean it's going to be dangerous." Zafira said.

"Please." Maya waved a dismissive hand. "I live for danger. I can handle myself." There was confidence in her voice.

"Well if you're sure. Let's go!" Zafira said and started to head out with Maya.

On their adventure, they did not know that they had people following them. The village that had helped Zafira was going to join in on the journey. They also wanted peace for the world they lived in. The villagers were willing to not only fight but die for a free world if need be. She had also become part of their family within the short amount of time that she had spent with them. They would not let her go into battle alone. They would fight by her side until the end.

While on the quest, Zafira looked back and noticed all the creatures that had joined them. She saw demons of all kinds, from Maya's village. She saw that not only Raidon had joined them, but she also saw wolf demons, some bird demons, some fairy demons just to name a few of the many different species that had also joined them. She was happy that she had people to help her fight this battle, but was she willing to have them die for her? No, she could not let that happen. Zafira stopped running causing everyone else to stop and look at her confused.

"No," Zafira said, making everyone even more confused than they already were.

"What do you mean no?" Maya asked.

"No, I will not let all of you die for me." Zafira raised her voice, so they all heard. "This is my mission, not yours!"

"We are going to fight in this battle! You can't stop us!" a wolf demon with short black hair, green eyes, and black wolf fur on his armor said.

"We will fight!" a fire demon said with grim determination in his voice. This demon had short red hair and red eyes with tints of orange in them. He looked to be no older than sixteen.

"After all, this is more than just your battle. We are fighting for our freedom as well." Another wolf demon said only this one had brown hair a little past his shoulders and blue eyes with brown wolf fur and red armor. He too, looked like he was just a teenager.

Zafira sighed. She had no idea what to do. She liked that she had help, but she was not willing to let any more innocent lives be lost. She looked at Maya for support in her decision, but Maya just nodded. Very well, if they wanted to help, they could, but she hoped with all she was worth that they remained safe.

"Fine, but everyone watch your backs and be prepared for anything. You may not make it out alive. Now let's go." Zafira looked over everyone, who all seemed to nod in understanding.

It would take a few days to get to Red Shadows, but she would destroy it and reclaim peace. She would make her parents proud. Zafira and the others stopped for the night. While the others slept, Zafira could not. She was too anxious and felt the need to keep her guard up. She was afraid that Lucios or one of his Blood Demons would jump out at any moment, so she stayed awake.

As Zafira watched the campfire in front of her crackle, she heard a twig snap off in the distance. She jumped quickly and turned around to see that it was just Raidon. She sighed in relief and turned back to face the fire as she heard the crinkling of the leaves and another branch snap as he sat next to her.

"Something on your mind?" Raidon asked her.

"I'm just trying to wrap my head around this whole situation still." She said with nervousness in her voice.

"It is a lot to take in I agree, but you have been training hard with me and you are ready. If we happen to lose this battle and must retreat, we will come back stronger than before. But I doubt that will happen." Raidon explained.

"How are you so confident in me, I mean with how you acted the first time we met I thought you hated me," Zafira said.

"I don't hate you, nor do I hate my fellow villagers, but I do have a grudge against Blood Demons and humans." Zafira saw Raidon, clench his fist as he mentioned the Blood Demons and humans.

"Why?"

"My mother was in the forest by the village one day, gathering some food for our hut. She didn't know that I had followed her. I saw a human come up behind her and before I could shout for her to watch out, he hit my mother on the back with a stick. She turned around and threw a powerful conjuring at him that caused him to fly back. She took the opportunity to try and escape, but the guy ran and tackled her and once he caught up to her, he drew a dagger from his side and thrust it deep into her chest. He then ripped her wings off and ran off leaving my mother's lifeless body."

She looked at Raidon in shock. She knew Maya had told her that he had lost his parents when he was young, but she never would have imaged something so horrific happening to him.

"I immediately ran back to my hut and told my father. Once I led him to the place where my mother was, he held her and shed some tears which was strange to see, my father was always this strict, stoic man. Once he got up, I saw such hatred in my father's eyes. He told me to stay with my mother and he ran off into the forest. I didn't know it at the time, but he had run off to hunt down the human that killed my mother. A few hours passed until he came back, but when he did, he lifted my mother into his arms, and we made our way back to the village and buried her. A few years later, I was hunting with my father and he was attacked by a few Blood Demons. He fought a good fight, but they were too much for him. So that's what happened to my parents. I know you lost your parents to the Blood Demons, but so have I and many others have as well. So, I know the hatred that burns in your heart for them, and I understand your need for vengeance. But you must let it empower you, not cloud your focus."

"I'm sorry Raidon."

"Don't be. If anything, when I lost both my parents, I became a lot stronger. Anyway, you should get some rest. I'll watch the camp," Raidon said and Zafira nodded at him and went to sleep.

The next morning, she ate something quickly to keep up her energy for the battle she knew lay ahead.

Once the village in Red Shadows was in sight, Zafira, Maya, Raidon and the rest of the group that had joined her hid behind the trees bordering Red Shadows. The village was dark, dreary, almost lifeless. There was nothing but darkness and a red moon lighting up the sky. The village consisted of small buildings constructed out of stone. Not your typical village. Everything was lifeless just how Blood Demons liked seeing their victims. There were Blood Demons lurking around every corner. Some were sitting around feeding on some humans they had recently hunted, while others were just goofing around with one another telling jokes and having a laugh. Some were just strolling through the village with some guards on duty. Zafira needed to think of a way to get past them and face Lucios. She needed to get to the main source of the Blood Demons and defeat him and then this would hopefully all be over. Zafira looked around and saw that the castle she was held captive in by Lucios was hidden in the distance by some trees.

"Maya. Can you, Raidon, and a few others create a distraction so I can get near the castle?" Zafira asked Maya.

"Sure. But what are you going to do?" Maya asked.

"I'm going to face Lucios," Zafira said, determined.

"Zafira, you cannot face him alone." Maya's brow furrowed. "Let me help you."

"This is something I need to do myself." Zafira started towards Lucios' castle but was stopped by her friend. Judging by the distance it looked like it would take a day or two to get there.

"Why do you have to be so stubborn?" Maya cried.

"It's just the way I am," Zafira said seriously. "This is my battle."

"You're not the only one with something at stake in this battle!" Maya said, but Zafira just ignored her.

Before she took off to the castle, she saw Maya jump out of the tree she was hiding in and throw a powerful blast of wind from her hands knocking some Blood Demons down.

"Raging Wind!" Maya shouted.

The Blood Demons were caught off guard but decided to fight back. Before the nearest Blood Demon could throw a counterattack at Maya, Zafira saw some wind form over her hand, and she punched the earth beneath her feet causing the ground to shake and throw some Blood Demons back.

"Wind Fist." Zafira heard Maya yell.

She was shocked at how powerful Maya's wind punch was, but she took it as an opportunity to start making her way towards the castle.

Along the way, she was shocked at what she saw beneath her as she ran through the trees. She was surprised that the Blood Demons hadn't picked up on her scent yet, but she was glad in a way. If they hadn't been alerted to her presence yet that meant that she could conserve her strength for fighting Lucios and not wasting it on these Blood Demons. Still, it pained Zafira at what she was seeing; there were many villages in the Red Shadows area that had been taken over by the Blood Demons, people were in chains while Blood Demons stood guard and forced them to work, the conditions were deplorable, there was very little food to feed the workers. Zafira could hardly bear the sight; if this had been the fate of her village instead of the total destruction the Blood Demons wrought; she didn't know how she would have reacted. *This is awful. I need to defeat Lucios quick!*

Many of the villagers had not only looked malnourished, but there were bruises on them as well. It looked as though they were being beaten if they did not work fast enough. Lucios had his guards taking control and making the villagers into his own personal army of slaves. If the villagers couldn't work anymore or fell and couldn't get up, the Blood Demons sucked them dry. This caused many of them to work fast, in fear of being a Blood Demon's next meal. Human or creature, it did not matter to them. Zafira hurried through these villages as best as she could to reach the castle. She was more determined now than ever to defeat Lucios and make him pay for his hideous crimes.

All the terrible things she saw brought back painful memories. All Zafira saw was red, the bloodstained grass, dead bodies of people she knew strewn everywhere like they were nothing more than dead weight. What if the villagers and her parents were still alive? Would they have been turned into slaves as well and drained of blood when they couldn't work anymore? It was too painful to even imagine. She would give anything to have those images erased from her mind. Zafira shook her head and snapped out of her horrible thoughts.

Once in sight, she headed towards the dark castle that belonged to the monster known as Lucios. He needed to pay. She knew she could never find it within herself to forgive him. Everyone deserved to be free regardless of what species they were.

She was snapped out of her thoughts as a Blood Demon flying above the castle suddenly swooped down at her throwing her off guard. The Blood Demon must have caught her scent since she was so close to the castle. *Darn it! There went the element of surprise,* the creature with its red eyes, dragon-like wings and sharp claws lunged at Zafira.

She fell to the ground but quickly recovered and felt fire slowly building up in the palm of her hand. Once the fire had formed to where she wanted it, she threw Eternal Scorch right at the Blood Demon and then leaped into the air to avoid another altercation. She didn't even turn back to look and see what became of the Blood Demon, time was of the essence now, she had to get to the castle before Lucios had time to escape.

Chapter Eight: Into the Castle

ONCE SHE HAD REACHED the castle midway, a lot more Blood Demons seemed to be milling around. She had a feeling that getting to the castle itself was going to be more of a challenge then she thought. But she was not going to waste any time. Any Blood Demon that got in her way, she was going to destroy.

"Out of my way!" Zafira yelled and shot a bolt of lightning at a Blood Demon. She had no time for their games. All she cared about was getting to Lucios and destroying him once and for all. The closer she got to the castle the more the adrenaline spiked in her veins.

She looked back and saw Maya had almost caught up to her and was fighting some Blood Demons with the help of some of the villagers. She saw all different types of conjures being thrown at the Blood Demons, everything from various element conjuring to magic strikes. She was going to have to repay them somehow. She saw Maya look back at her with a nod as if assuring her to continue; she had this covered and would catch up as soon as she was able. She saw Maya throw a Wind Kick at a Blood Demon and then Zafira continued to the castle. Hoping that her friend would be alright, she then moved onward towards the castle that was finally within seeing distance. *I owe you one Maya. Just stay safe. Please.*

Zafira ran as fast she could, along the way the trees that were once so filled with life were replaced with nothing but dead ones. The lifeless vegetation surrounding her only saddened her further. The Blood Demons were doing more than destroying humans, they were destroying nature itself. Zafira was finally faced with the castle of a monster as she approached the castle doors. The castle exterior was a dark, dreary, grey color. It was held together by stone and had a gate made of metal at the entrance with guards surrounding it. There were multiple chambers from what Zafira could see from the outside. There was barely anything living surrounding the castle except for a few dead trees. The castle was brightened by a dark red sun that almost looked like the color of blood. Lucios was within her reach and she could sense it. A tingling chill ran down her spine as she thought about what was about to take place. She was frightened but would not let it show. She had to be brave. This was it. She was ready to face the monster who caused so much pain. *It is time to pay for all that you have done. You are finished destroying lives.*

THE WOOD SPLINTERED from her lightning, and she threw more at the guards who'd been alerted to her presence. She had no time for these fools. She only wanted one thing: to end Lucios.

She slammed her hands into the stony castle floor and rocks sprouted from the ground and headed towards the guards, pelting them until they fell to the ground disabled. Once they were taken care of, Zafira raced upstairs in search of Lucios.

A laugh echoed throughout the castle, but he was nowhere in sight. Darn it! Where was he? She was done with games!

"Lucios! Show yourself you coward!" Blood felt like it was boiling inside of her veins at the thought of his poisonous name slipping past her lips.

Zafira then heard Lucios' menacing laugh echoing throughout the castle once more. The sound gave her goosebumps and made her body shake with fear, but she refused to let her fear get the best of her. His laugh reminded Zafira of an animal dying and writhing in pain. She glanced around to see if she could find where the laugh had come from, but she saw no one; there was no trace of anyone in the near vicinity. Was he seriously mocking her?

"Now where's the fun in that?" The monster's voice reverberated up the staircase where she stood. "If you want to face me then you have to find me," Lucios shouted.

"This isn't a game!" Frustration rose up strongly in Zafira, making her clench her fist and grind her teeth together as Lucios toyed with her.

"Oh yes, it is," Lucios' tone was as smug as ever. "You see, Zafira, for each hour that you don't find me, someone will die."

"Lucios!"

She clenched her fists tighter, digging her nails into her skin. Zafira needed to find where he was hiding and fast, she could not let Maya or anyone else die.

Lucios would suffer as she and so many others had—it would be slow, painful. Once he was gone, everything would be tranquil once more.

Even if it proved a difficult task, she was determined to do this. To him, this might have been just a game, but to Zafira, this was a mission—a mission to restore the world to a peaceful place filled with happiness and laughter, not fear and despair.

Chapter Nine: Searching for Lucios

SPRINTING THROUGH THE halls, Zafira was determined not to give Lucios the chance to hurt anyone else. She searched the high end of the castle as well as the low, but there was no sign of him anywhere. He had to be somewhere, but where?

Running her hands along the walls as she went through the corridor, she felt for any unusual markings that could possibly lead to a trapdoor or secret room. She had searched almost every space in the castle, so this was her last-ditch effort. However, nothing seemed out of the ordinary. It looked like a regular castle. The walls were made of stone and had pictures along the walls of other members of the royal family.

Probably ancestors from a long time ago. There were a few chandeliers hanging from the ceiling with some torches illuminating the walls with light. The walls felt solid, not hollow at all indicating no such detail that there were some hidden rooms concealed with these walls. With how sneaky and cruel the Blood Demons were, she wouldn't be surprised if they were hiding a torture chamber or dungeon of some sort somewhere in the castle.

Zafira felt upwards, frustrated because she hadn't found anything. She was running out of time and she could not let Lucios kill anyone else. She wouldn't be able to bear it if another person she cared about died. Zafira had already lost her parents and fellow villagers; she wasn't about to lose her best friend and the creatures of Maya's village as well.

Pausing, Zafira took a deep breath to collect herself. Getting frustrated would get her nowhere. She had to remain calm and collected, even if she wanted to rip Lucios' head off. After all, she remembered what her parents said: if she got frustrated, it would only result in her losing control and Lucios would be able to defeat her.

Just then she heard a young female screaming in agony. She knew that voice but could not place who it was. Zafira sprinted as fast as she could to where she heard the scream. *Wait a second. That was Maya!* Zafira picked up her pace, running faster than her legs would carry her. Zafira followed the sound of Maya's never-ending screams to an open black door with a gold trim and gold handle. The room in the castle looked like a dungeon, with many tools of torture. Lucios stood in plain sight, not even attempting to hide from her.

The room before Zafira had chains along the walls, holding up some villagers, including Maya. The room was lit by torches hanging along the wall. There were cobwebs hanging from corners of the ceiling. The floor was stone cold, like ice. There was a little table in the corner, with some items on it, but since she couldn't see what they were she just assumed they were instruments of torture that had been used on Maya and the villagers. Zafira saw Lucios, he had his back turned to her, looking at a beaten-up Maya, and some of the villagers looked as if they had suffered the same fate as well. They must have been through a lot, bruises and cuts covered their bodies, some even had blood dripping down their faces.

"Hello, Zafira," Lucios said turning around to face Zafira with a smug look. "I see your precious friend here got your attention."

Zafira looked at Lucios and saw that he was wearing his usual black pants, with black boots and a red t-shirt, that showed off his defined chest. He also wore a black cape, with some jewels on the shoulders of the cape. His hair falling over his shoulders slightly and the jewelry on his hands and neck indicated that he was royalty. It was as if Lucios was trying to show off his superior status to her. Proving, that he was indeed better than her, or anyone in that matter.

From what it seemed like Maya still seemed to appear unbroken. Her spirit seemed to still be intact as she threw a smile at Zafira, though she could tell it was painful for her. Still, seeing her best friend injured and in pain, made her thirst for revenge. The blood in her body heated up and her body started to heat up from the aggression she was feeling inside. Zafira let out a scream of frustration.

Zafira's eyes blazed with fury and unshed tears. "You will pay dearly for this!"

A surge of energy crashed through her body. Maya had been nothing but kind to her and Zafira was going to make Lucios pay for all the cruel things he had done. The anger increased more and more, as she saw Maya and the villagers let out groans of pain.

"You are going to experience a pain like no other for your crimes Lucios!" Zafira yelled in anger.

Lucios laughed. "Try if you wish! I'm not afraid of a weak, pathetic, little girl. You can't hurt me."

"Do not underestimate me!"

Her markings began to glow a bright yellow, and Zafira could feel the immense power she held within her run through her veins. The burning she had felt in her body earlier had intensified and it really felt as if her body was on fire. She felt herself becoming stronger as she thought of Lucios hurting her friends. Zafira let out a scream mixed with pain and frustration as she threw a powerful fire explosion at where Lucios stood. The flame appeared as a medium-sized fire ball and once it hit where Lucios stood it caused the room to fill with smoke, but once it cleared, she did not see the monster anywhere.

That was too easy. There was no way he could have been destroyed so soon.

"IS THAT ALL YOU'VE really got?" Lucios mocked hiding in the corner of the ceiling, unknown to Zafira. While she glanced frantically around the room, in search of Lucios, he took the opportunity and made Maya and the villagers disappear to another dungeon with the snap of his fingers.

"I was expecting more of a challenge from you, Zafira. Your parents would be ashamed if they were still alive." With that last word, Lucios disappeared once more.

TEARS FILLED HER EYES. "Shut up!"

How dare he mention her parents. It was his fault they were dead! He was to blame for their deaths and her misery.

Scanning the room, she yelled in frustration. Zafira felt as if she had betrayed her friend by letting Lucios get to her and hurt her. Her body had felt drained not from fighting Lucios, but all the pain he had caused her and her loved ones. He had slipped through her fingers. She gritted her teeth and punched a wall as she thought of how he had once more escaped like vapor in the breeze. She wiped the tears that she could feel falling down her face from sadness, frustration, and pain. This was no time to cry, she had to try and find Lucios once more.

Calm. Stay calm. Getting frustrated will only make things harder.

Once she had collected herself, Zafira began her search once again through the dark, dreary castle. She was once again getting nowhere. Zafira had searched every room once more and found the same as she had the first time: nothing. However, one of the walls felt strange. One of them seemed to have a softer texture than the rest. She tapped it a few times; it sounded hollow, different from the rest. Zafira took a few steps back and threw a ball of fire towards it.

Amid the rubble settling, a stairwell appeared. It was lit with torches along the walls, and the only sound that could be heard was water dripping from the ceiling.

Grabbing one of the many torches, she carefully made her way down the stairs of the creepy hall. With each step she took, Zafira could feel the fear in her body increasing, but she wasn't about to let it show. She just had to be brave if not for herself, then for the others who were counting on her—Maya, her parents, and those fighting for their freedom. She wanted to be brave. No, she *needed* to be brave.

With that thought in mind, she had reached the end of the stairs and came to a black door with red handles and drippings that looked like blood. The door also had gold trim around the outside of it. The dripping design of blood started from the bottom and stopped midway up the door. The design of the door made her cringe as she thought of her parents and those who had been killed because of these monsters. Her hand shook as it moved towards the handle.

Wait. What was she doing? Why was she shaking in fear? She had to be confident and fierce. She could not be a coward. Reassuring herself, Zafira opened the door and entered the room beyond.

"Nice of you to finally join us Zafira," Lucios said with a smirk.

Zafira's eyes widen at the sight before her. Maya was chained tightly up against a wall along with about twenty others that had gone into battle against the Blood Demons. Many of the others had seemed to avoid being captured. About a hundred demons had gone into battle with Zafira and only a small portion had been captured thankfully.

"Let them go!" Zafira demanded.

"Why would I do something like that?" Lucios asked with raised eyebrows.

Maya screamed, interrupting their exchange. Zafira watched her friend squirm in pain. What was Lucios doing to her? He didn't look like he had attacked her, so what was he doing? It didn't look like he was currently conjuring her. She couldn't sense any magic in the room.

"I see that you're angry Zafira. What you don't like my fancy chains for your friends?" Lucios said with all too familiar smirk.

"What do you mean fancy chains?" Zafira said with hatred for Lucios clear in her voice. The chains her friends wore look liked plain old regular chains. They were silver and long, but a bit rusted. They didn't look fancy at all. So, why did Maya scream then?

"You see, my dear Zafira," Lucios chuckled, "these chains have the ability to send an electric shock throughout their bodies whenever I want them to. Now which of your friends should be the first to die?"

"You monster!" Zafira bellowed. "I'll make you regret doing such a thing! And I won't let any of my friends die by the likes of you!"

Glaring at Lucios, she felt the power building within her. Her body felt as if it grew heavier, but she was still able to stand her ground. Zafira ignored the familiar burning pain in her body as her rage towards Lucios caused each element to increase in strength.

"I will make you pay Lucios!" Zafira roared.

He laughed in response. "Go ahead and try, little girl."

Zafira was getting tired of his attitude. She'd had enough of everything and just wanted this to be over. For the pain to stop and the peace to return. That would only happen if she could defeat Lucios and free her friends.

Chapter Ten: The Fight

THERE WAS A COLD BREEZE as Zafira and Lucios' eyes met. Both were waiting for the other to make the first move, but no one did—maybe a flinch of the hand, but that was it.

"Well, princess," Lucios mocked, "what are you going to do?"

"Do not call me princess!"

When her fists contacted the tile beneath her feet, it began to crumble. She was hoping Lucios would lose his balance, but unfortunately, she had no such luck. He just jumped out of the way, showing off by doing a flip in the process.

"You missed," he said once he'd landed. "Why don't you try again?"

This only angered Zafira as she ran at Lucios and just when she was about to attack him, she grabbed him by the shoulder and threw him over hers. The adrenaline her anger provided had built up so much that she was shocked at how easily she had grabbed him like that. She was not expecting that to happen, but the anger in her body had gotten the best of her. Lucios managed to catch himself before he hit the wall behind him.

"Not bad for a girl," Lucios joked.

Holding out her hands, Zafira felt the electrical energy running through them. She concentrated so the power in her hands would build up. The burning feeling ran from her arms all the way down to her hands, until there were yellow flashes of lighting leaving her hands. The detonation was so intense that it caused not only dust to appear, but it also caused the castle to shake a little. She had to be careful if she didn't want to injure her friends. Thinking that the bolts of lightning hit Lucios, Zafira smirked. The smirk was wiped from her face though as soon as she heard Lucios' voice.

"Careful, Zafira," Lucios warned, dusting himself off. "You wouldn't want the castle to cave in, now would you?"

He was right. What was she to do? *Come on think!* Zafira thought.

Once more she threw another lightning blast at Lucios. The electricity had caused an explosion giving Zafira the opportunity to go over to Maya. Once she was by Maya's side, she had built up enough electricity in her hand forming a blade and cut Maya's chains.

Zafira whispered in her ear, "I am going to lead him away. I wanted to tell you, so you don't think I just left you."

Maya nodded with understanding. "Go ahead," she whispered. "I'll handle things here. Teach that monster a lesson."

Zafira then turned around, the smoke from her lightning had finally cleared and Lucios stood before her. She quickly scanned the room but didn't see any exits except for the door that she had come in before. As Zafira looked back at Lucios, she quickly felt her hand burn and turn a dark red. She then flung a ball of red, orange, and yellow fire at Lucios. While it caused an eruption, she then took the chance to run around the fire and out the door of the dungeon.

"Ah, I see right through your little game. I always love a good chase." Lucios said as he grinned evilly.

Zafira took a glance at Lucios as he revealed his wings as he appeared from the dungeon, following behind her. The wings on his back were large and scaly like a dragon. They were black and looked to have a rough texture. As she looked back, she noticed something in his eye. It was a sparkle of some kind. As if the chase made him ecstatic somehow. That thought sent a shiver down her spine. This looked like it was just game to Lucios, from what she could tell. This was more than a game though. It was a battle of life and death and it had barely even begun.

Zafira glanced back and noticed that she was ahead of Lucios. She could see him in the distance, flying throughout the castle trying to keep his eyes peeled for her. Lucios seemed like the type of demon who had fun playing around with his victims, but she was not going to be one. She didn't know it yet, but she had many other powers just waiting to be discovered.

"Zafira, come out, come out wherever you are," Lucios practically sang.

The sun was setting, and Zafira who had managed to make it outside of the castle hid in the shadows alongside one of the castle walls as Lucios passed over her. Once she was sure he hadn't spotted her, she slid out from the corner of the castle she was hiding in. She concentrated and powered up a fireball and aimed it at Lucios, but it barely burned him as he dodged her once more and she groaned in frustration. If she was ever to defeat him, Zafira needed to figure out Lucios' weakness. She had yet to find one. She refused to give up, conjuring any element she could think of, but he only flew out of the way. *Darn it! Not one single attack had hit him!*

She was at a disadvantage with Lucios' flight abilities. How was she going to defeat him if she couldn't fly? Right now, it seemed as if Lucios had the upper hand and she did not like that at all. She wished she could fly as well, maybe then this battle would be on a little more even footing.

She was so into her thoughts that she was barely able to dodge a ball of shadows, the attack was swirling orbs of black darkness, nothing but shadow from what she could tell.

"Dark Chaos!" Zafira heard Lucios call out in anger.

Zafira sighed in relief as she managed to dodge its impact. She would never survive this battle if she did not concentrate on the task at hand: destroying Lucios. Zafira glanced around but did not see Lucios anywhere, so where did the attack come from? Where was he? She glanced around once more and spotted him right in the sky coming out from behind a dying tree.

Zafira suddenly threw a gust of wind at Lucios, hoping she could knock him out of the sky.

"Wind Raid," Zafira exclaimed.

At first, it appeared to work, but he recovered quickly and flew higher than before, managing to move away from the strong breeze. Zafira groaned as Lucios easily dodged her every attempt.

Concentrate. Concentrate. You will never defeat him if you continue to just throw blasts of every element at him like it is nothing. Think. Think.

Zafira closed her eyes and concentrated. *Wings. Wings.* That was Zafira's only thought, blocking Lucios out of her mind. *Wings.* The only thought running through her mind.

She felt a power that was unfamiliar to her surge through her body. Her body didn't feel like it was burning, it felt tight and rigid. She felt a painful tightness in her back, causing her skin to feel like it was tearing in half. She let out a scream as something grew on her back, ripping the top of her dress. When she opened her eyes, she looked behind her to see that a pair of light brown wings with white outlining on them had appeared. They also had white spots along the back. The wings appeared to go almost down to her knees. Zafira could not believe her eyes. *I can't believe it. I have wings.* They reminded her of an owl. The sacred animal of her village. Her village was known to care about all types of animals, from what her father had told her when she was younger, but owls were their most precious animals. They were a symbol of good luck and believed to ward off evil.

She was hoping that now since she too had the ability of flight; that would make it that much easier to defeat Lucios. Her body felt heavier, but she regained her balance. Zafira jumped up and was shocked that her wings cooperated with her.

"You honestly think that just because you have wings now that you can defeat me? I hate to disappoint you sweetheart, but you cannot beat me. I am invincible and once you are out of the picture. Each creature, mythical and human alike is going to be slaves to the Blood Demons. Soon the Blood Demons will rule this world!"

What Lucios said, fueled Zafira's anger as she clenched her fist and let out a scream of anger. Zafira glanced around, but she couldn't see Lucios anywhere. He was hiding like a coward. She scanned the outside of the castle, but she did not see Lucios. Where was he?

"That's what you think you cruel, blood-sucking, hideous monster!" She yelled throughout the entire forest. Next thing she knew Lucios appeared right in front of her shocking Zafira? How did he do that? She hadn't even heard him move.

"Such foul words from such a pretty, *tasty*, looking mouth," Lucios said with his familiar grin appearing on his cruel face.

She ignored his comment, recovered from her shock and lunged forward ready to punch him, but he slipped out of the way. This caused her to stumble a bit in the air, but she quickly regained her balance. She had barely touched him. Quickly recovering, Zafira swung a powerful roundhouse kick towards Lucios' chest before he had time to react. The impact of the kick was so powerful that it sent Lucios flying through a wall. Zafira smiled, satisfied as she gained speed and sprinted in his direction. She tried to land a punch on Lucios, but he quickly dodged it before she could hit him.

As Zafira flew in the sky and threw hit after hit, nothing made a scratch. Even with these new wings of hers, she still could not manage to hit Lucios. Each time she flew at him to attack, he would quickly evade it.

Was she not quick enough? Had these new wings of hers slowed her down? She didn't know, but she had to figure something out.

If she did not come up with something quick, this fight would never end, and she would never be able to save anybody. She wished her parents were still here so they could guide her. Right now, the task seemed impossible.

Please, Mother, her mind cried out. *Please, Father. Please give me the strength I need.*

Zafira then closed her eyes. As she concentrated, everything seemed to slow down. She felt a warm feeling run up her shoulder. It was as if someone was touching her. Zafira slowly opened her eyes and turned to look behind her. She saw the ghost of her mother, giving her an encouraging smile. This shocked Zafira, she closed her eyes, only to reopen them to see nothing there. She suddenly felt more confident though for some reason, but she couldn't explain why. Nothing else seemed to matter, not Lucios or his fellow Blood Demons. Then suddenly, a bright light shone, blinding Lucios.

Fading Light. Zafira thought as light surrounded her and helped her disappear.

Zafira took the opportunity to briefly retreat so she could think of a plan. She had found a spot to hide in the forest, where there was still signs of life, away from Lucios' castle. As she landed on a tree to rest Zafira admired her wings once more.

She felt upset with herself for running away and she felt like a terrible friend, like she had just abandoned Maya and the others, but she hoped they would understand why she had to do what was she was about to do. Although, Maya was strong from what she had seen, and she was sure that Maya would forgive her. Once she had run a good distance away, she sat down and tried to catch her breath. She glanced back from where she had come and it looked like Lucios hadn't had followed her, thankfully. Battling with the Blood Demon had taken a toll on her body, and she needed to restore her strength before she faced off with him again. Closing her eyes, Zafira rested; she was tired, the more she gave in to the world fading around her, the pain began to fade as well.

Chapter Eleven: Zafira Sees Her Parents

ZAFIRA'S EYES WIDENED as she woke to a bright light hitting her face. How long had she been asleep? *Oh no! What was I thinking?* So many scenarios raced through her head that she didn't know what to do next. From what Zafira could tell, Lucios was sensitive to light. Maybe, she could use that to her advantage. All she had to do was figure out the right elemental technique to use.

She rested her head on her knees, lost in thought. Just when everything seemed impossible, a light flashed before her eyes. Once her vision had cleared, standing before her stood the ghosts of her parents. She could not believe that they were standing here before her once more.

"Mom. Dad." Zafira said so softly that you could barely hear it.

Once she stood before them, she wanted so badly to hug her mother and father—cry into their arms. Seeing them was enough.

"Zafira," Ryker said as he looked at his daughter with such love in his eyes.

Zafira watched as tears streaked down her mother's face. All she wanted right then was to just be able to reach her hand out and wipe the tears off her mother's face, but what was the point?

"Mom, Dad, what do I do? Defeating Lucios is impossible." She fought the urge to cry, wanting to be strong for them.

"Zafira, do not give up, dear," her mother said. "You have the power to defeat him; you just have to believe in yourself."

"How though? How am I supposed to defeat someone who appears to be resistant to every element I throw at him!" Frustration building up in Zafira's voice.

Zafira took a deep breath, slowly releasing it from her lungs. Once she was sure she had calmed down, she turned her attention back to her parents.

"Zafira! Calm down!" Ryker said at his daughter, raising his voice slightly.

Zafira then closed her eyes and took a deep breath and let it out. Once she was sure she had calmed down Zafira opened her eyes once more and looked at her parents. She waited in silence for her parents to say something, anything that might help her defeat Lucios. She just needed their guidance on the situation she was currently in. She needed their guidance to reassure her that every-thing was going to work out alright in the end.

"What did you notice when you were battling Lucios?" Zafira heard her father ask.

His question confused her. "What do you mean?"

"What your father means," Zafira's mother explained, "is were there any faults in the way he moved? Did he have any weaknesses? Did he move slower when he was on the surface rather than flying? Those sorts of details might just be what we need to know. Your father and I can only help you so much though. This is your battle and you alone must fight it. Do you understand what we are saying, Zafira?"

"I mean..." she thought a moment. "Lucios was quicker when he was flying, but when he was on the ground fighting with me, he was a bit slower. The only element that seemed to hurt him was light—all the other elements seemed use-less."

"There is your answer," Zafira heard her mother say.

"What's the answer?" She still didn't grasp what they were saying. "Fighting him on the ground?"

"Yes," her father confirmed. "You must fight him in a secluded area with walls that are low and use mainly light attacks. If you do this, then you should be able to defeat him." Her father postulated.

"But what if that doesn't work?" Zafira asked. "Then what?"

"It will, my daughter," Sophina reassured her. "You just have to believe. Do as we instructed, and if for some reason that does not work, think of us and we will come."

"I will," she promised. "If you both are with me, there is no way I won't de-feat Lucios."

"That's the spirit," Ryker praised.

"Good luck, Zafira," Sophina said. "We love you."

"You can avenge our deaths." Ryker smiled. "We believe in you."

Zafira's parents disappeared just as easily as they had come. It probably wasn't the smartest idea, but she wanted to lead Lucios away from the castle and the others to a more secluded area as her parents suggested. Ready to fight again, she had faith in her parents' advice as she headed back to the monster's lair. If their suggestions didn't work, she would think of another plan. Giving up was not an option.

She ran back in the direction she had come from towards the castle. What seemed like an hour was only forty-five minutes by the time she had arrived at the castle once more. Once the castle was in sight, Zafira ran up to the entrance and began her journey through the now nearly destroyed castle.

Fear was shoved in the back of her mind as she made her way into the castle; the only thing she was concerned about was finally restoring peace to Moon Shine and all the other villages. Most importantly, Zafira was determined to avenge her parents' deaths.

Chapter Twelve: The Chase

IT WAS QUIET, TOO QUIET. Zafira kept her guard up as she scanned her surroundings. Everything in the castle looked the same except for the parts that were destroyed from her previous battle with Lucios. Zafira didn't realize how much of an impact her conjures had; a lot of damage had been done. The walls looked partially destroyed, with parts of stone crumbling. One of the balconies of the castle appeared to be disintegrating. She slowly, quietly stalked the halls, keeping an eye out for Lucios. As she walked along the castle, she noticed some of the interior had also been destroyed, probably from the battle she had with Lucios.

Just as she was coming up on a dimly lit hallway, she was tackled to the floor. It was as if some type of immovable force had thrown her to the ground. She looked around but nothing appeared out of order. What could have attacked her? Just then Zafira was pushed to the ground and pinned down with her back lying on the floor. She was caught off guard by the sudden assault. Zafira looked up to see Lucios holding her arms down with his hands and his face right in hers.

"Surprise!" Lucios yelled as he continued to pin Zafira down.

"Get off!" Zafira thrust her knee upward striking Lucios in the crotch.

"You wench!" He gasped as he fell to the ground beside her.

Getting to her feet, Zafira fixed Lucios with a mischievous glare. If he wanted to play games, she would play games as well. She wouldn't make this easy for him.

She stuck out her tongue and taunted, "Catch me if you can!"

Zafira didn't dare look back as she sprinted. She had to get Lucios away from the castle, and that was all that mattered. Zafira ran towards the exit knowing Lucios would follow her if he wanted to hunt her down so badly.

Just then a blast came up from behind her. It was so powerful it knocked her down, dust clouding the air. She coughed as it cleared and hopped back into a jog, picking up her pace.

Zafira ran as far as her feet could carry her and she couldn't stop yet; she wasn't far enough away. If the castle was in sight, Lucios would still have the upper hand. Zafira raced for what seemed like hours, searching for an area she could trap him. As she looked around, she noticed that she was mainly surrounded by woods. Lucios could easily evade her if he wanted to, but he wasn't the only one who could fly now. She could fly as well, but how could she gain the upper hand? She needed to find some way to defeat Lucios who would probably catch up to her soon.

She dared not look back though, afraid that she would come face to face with Lucios. If that were to happen, then reality would sink in: she was in a dangerous battle for her life and many other creatures that depended on her to win.

"You can't get away from me that easily, little Zafira." Lucios' cackle echoed through the woods—he was enjoying their chase too much.

"I'm not so little!" Zafira rapidly turned and threw a Fire Bloom in Lucios' direction. Everything in the forest shook from the eruption she had inflicted. Before the smoke could clear the area, Zafira took advantage of her opportunity to escape.

She felt the branches beneath her feet, heard them snap with each step she took. She moved quickly, hiding behind a tree to catch her breath. She had been running for so long that she was starting to lose her energy. Because she was doing her best to lure Lucios away from the castle and her friends, she'd forgotten that she could fly. Zafira took the opportunity to close her eyes and thought of her wings. She felt the familiar tightness in her back as they emerged from behind her.

"Surprise!" Lucios said with a laugh as he popped out from behind a tree with his dragon-like wings.

Zafira jumped but sent Eternal Scorch at him and broke into a flight. She looked around and changed directions, moving branches out of the way as they lashed her skin. She ignored Lucios as he continued to mock her. She needed to find some type of cave where she would have the advantage; there had to be one around here somewhere.

"Come out and play, Zafira!" Lucios called.

She saw a cave up ahead and took advantage of the opportunity and bolted for it. The cave appeared to be a dark grey color with an uneven shape to it. She flew as fast as her wings would carry her, despite her exhaustion. Once, she was close enough to the cave she flew inside and took cover. She held her breath as she rested against a wet rock. The floor beneath her feet was wet and musty. She did not care though. She was just hoping that this cave would give her an advantage against Lucios.

As she tucked herself against the wall, Zafira could hear water dripping from the ceiling. Peeking from behind the rock, she didn't see Lucios anywhere. She took advantage of the quiet moment and walked further into the cave, each step causing the water beneath her feet to ripple. The cave was dark, damp, and cold inside. All she could hear were the echoes of water steadily dripping into larger pools on the cave floor.

For what seemed like miles, there was nothing but bland, wet rocks. The cave itself didn't appear sturdy. If she was to throw even one element at Lucios the structure would surely collapse and trap them both. She would have to be careful. The rocks of the cave had some cracks along the walls and the roof of the cave. It was as if some horrible storm or tornado of some kind had destroyed the structure of it. She would have to think about how she threw her attacks and what kind she would use against Lucios.

Zafira continued along the narrow passageway and came to rest at what looked like two different entrances. She did not know which one to take. Neither tunnel looked pleasing to her eye, and there was no right answer written out in front of her. There was something pulling her towards the left entrance though, so Zafira followed her gut and walked through.

She had no idea what was down the path she'd chosen, but Zafira wasn't going to be afraid. If she was brave enough to fight Lucios, then she was brave enough to walk through a dark, creepy-looking cave.

Turning her head slightly, she made sure she hadn't been followed. *Could he have gotten lost? No. That was too easy. He was probably waiting to pop out when she least expected it.*

The tunnel opened up to a space that was exactly as her parents described it. The ceiling was low, and it was well secluded. This would be the perfect way to ensure Lucios' demise. The low ceiling would give her an advantage since he probably wouldn't be able to fly as freely. Neither would she, but she was used to using her feet. Lucios, on the other hand seemed as if it was a struggle for him. She believed she would clearly have the upper hand.

"Here you are!" Lucios yelled.

Zafira quickly turned around to come face to face with the devil demon himself. He wore his fancy clothes that showed off his royal status with his dragon-like wings proudly extended on his back. She could see his fangs glistening in the dim light from the cave as he smiled wickedly at her. Zafira clenched her fist tightly and gritted her teeth with anger. A soft wind flew through the cave as they waited to see who would make the first move.

Chapter Thirteen: The Cave

IF ZAFIRA THOUGHT TIME was moving slowly before, then it felt like it had come to a complete standstill now. This was the Blood Demon who had caused so many people misery—herself included. This monster was the reason everyone in her village was dead. Her parents were dead because of him. She only hoped that Maya, Raidon, and the others who had willingly gone into battle with her did not suffer the same fate. Last she saw Raidon had been battling with Maya and some others.

"Lucios," Zafira said with as much hate as she could muster in her voice.

"So, Zafira," he said with a laugh. "You run all that way from the castle just to come to this gloomy cave? What an interesting choice."

"This is where I am going to defeat you."

She felt her blood boil and the power inside of her rise. Anger built up inside of Zafira as Lucios spoke. Her body felt like it was heating up hotter than usual. Zafira didn't fully understand why she was feeling this way but believed it had something to do with her powers. The markings on Zafira's right wrist started to glow and her wings emerged from behind her back. She was prepared to fight. This battle would end soon—she would make sure of it; there was no need to carry it out longer than necessary.

"You honestly think you can?

"Why don't you stop talking and battle me so that you can find out," Zafira said with a smirk.

"Bring it on," Lucios said determined to beat Zafira.

"Gladly." She lunged at the monster who had ruined her life.

All she felt was sadness and anger, her vision blocked by a blanket of red. She wanted to make Lucios pay; make him experience a slow, painful death.

Lucios moved out of the way and kneed Zafira in the gut. The impact not only hurt, but it sent her flying. Zafira ended up hitting her back against the hard wall of the cave, but she stood and caught her breath. She was far from done.

"You call this a battle? I call this an embarrassment." Lucios' laughter filled the cave.

"I'm just getting started!" Zafira yelled with a fiery look of determination in her eyes.

She could do this; she would not let Lucios get the best of her. Zafira would show him who was truly the weak one, and it wasn't her.

Zafira's body started to heat up more as her power raged through her and she felt this immense surge of energy rise inside of her. Her body, as usual, felt as if it was on fire, burning her from the inside, but she fought through the pain. She looked at Lucios with so much hate that the heat from the burning inside of her grew stronger. The outcome wouldn't be the same as last time. She would make sure of it.

Lucios leaped at Zafira and hurled his black shadow ball called Dark Chaos at her, which she quickly dodged. She spun around and threw her technique Lightning Blade at him, which knocked him off his feet. With caution, she approached the spot where the light had struck, thinking that it had hit him, but Zafira was unsure. It had to have hit him, right? She had to keep her guard up though; there was no telling what type of tricks Lucios was planning to pull. Since from what Zafira had learned about Lucios, he enjoyed playing games.

"Seems that you are the weak one, Lucios," Zafira said.

She expected to see him injured on the damp ground with a few scratches, but as soon at the dust cleared her eyes widened in shock. He was nowhere in sight. *Where could he have gone? He couldn't have just vanished, could he?* She looked around in every possible direction she could think of but saw nothing.

"Surprise!" she'd barely heard him shout as he tackled her to the floor, jolting her out of her thoughts.

When Zafira got up, he had disappeared once more. Her gaze frantically searched every inch of the cave, but he had slipped away. Zafira stayed on alert, but nothing appeared out of the ordinary. How was he doing this? She was losing her patience with his little game.

Just then she felt a pressure on her back and fell to her knees. She had been hit again, but she didn't see it. How was Lucios doing this? He was nowhere to be seen, but right now he had the upper hand. Frustrated with this whole situation, she had to consciously tell herself to calm down. Displaying any sort of irritation would only make him enjoy this more.

Zafira could hear his laugh taunting her. His laugh still had that evil tone to it that used to send chills down her spine, but now it just made her angry. She was not afraid anymore, she was braver. Lucios wouldn't—no he didn't scare her anymore. Glancing around she kept her eyes peeled, he didn't sound far judging from his laugh, he had to be somewhere nearby. She couldn't let him get the best of her. *Breathe in and out and concentrate. Concentrate.* Zafira opened her eyes and took a deep breath. She was ready. No more games. It was time to get serious.

Sensing something behind her, she turned around in time to catch Lucios about to throw a black and purple ball of darkness at her.

"Night Destruction!" She could hear the rage in Lucios' voice as he shouted his conjure.

Zafira held out her hand and slowly took a deep breath before she closed her eyes. She remembered when she was training with Raidon, how he had said that light is the biggest weakness of Blood Demons if it was powerful enough. Light. Light. Light. This was the only thing on her mind.

"Heavenly Destiny."

Zafira opened her eyes and as she saw Lucios coming closer and her hand started to glow with a diffused yellow light and a sphere of light left her hand, causing an explosion as the two collided with each other. The impact of the attack had caused Zafira to slide back a little, but she quickly recovered and stood her ground as the earth beneath her feet and the inside of the cave shook. The pressure wasn't great enough for the cave to collapse though. The smoke cleared, and the two enemies were face to face with each other, each completely unharmed. The tension in the cave grew thin as they stared each other down. Each other's hatred for one another burning in both of their eyes.

She threw a Lightning Blade at Lucios, who easily dodged it. He countered with Dark Chaos, but she flew out of the way as best as she could with the low ceiling.

Zafira threw Heavenly Destiny at Lucios, but he matched her with another Dark Chaos. The collision caused clouds of dirt to rain down from the ceiling and the cave to shake. Lucios used this chance to disappear again. Losing sight of him broke her concentration. *Think. Think. How is he doing that?* She looked around the cave, but she saw nothing except for wet rocks and shadows. *Wait! That's it! Shadows! Lucios can control shadows!*

Let's see how this battle ends now. But what can I do? I mean, now that I know what he's been doing there has to be something. Think, Zafira. Think, or Lucios will beat you.

In order to avoid any impending attack, Zafira recklessly shot off elements in every direction. She hoped she would at least get one hit in, but her attempts proved futile. Lucios, who hid in the shadows, just chuckled. He was having too much fun.

She continued to lose her temper and throw blast after blast everywhere. After throwing about two more blasts Zafira stopped. She fell to her knees exhausted, trying to catch her breath. This whole battle was starting to seem pointless. *Why?! Why couldn't she defeat Lucios? What was she missing? Yes, she got that he could hide in shadows, but how could she defeat that with light?*

Zafira closed her eyes and took a deep breath. She suddenly felt calmer. The breathing had once more calmed her down like it had done many times before. The anger she had earlier seemed to no longer cloud her mind or judgment. The only thing on her mind was finding Lucios, all the other thoughts in her mind had left. She then started to float into the air. She opened her eyes and concentrated hard on finding Lucios.

Seeing Darkness.

Zafira felt this power in her and glanced around the cave walls. It was as if she had inherited the ability to look through shadows. The once dark shadows that had inhabited the walls had now seemed a little brighter. The shadows were not as dark as they had once been. Her parents were right. All she had to do was concentrate and believe in herself. She spotted the outline of Lucios up in the far-right corner of the cave. She knew it was him because she could see an outline made of light in the cave and Lucios was the only other one in this cave. A smirk made its way across her face as she looked right at him.

Zafira had the advantage and she would prove it. Lucios was going to meet his demise. He just didn't know it was so soon.

Chapter Fourteen: Discovered

ZAFIRA TOOK A DEEP breath and concentrated. She mustered up a Heavenly Destiny and threw it where she could see Lucios hovering in midair, whose eyes widened in shock. He just barely avoided the strike. The light had collided with part of the cave interior. Once the smoke had cleared from the explosion, Zafira saw that Heavenly Destiny had left a big hole in the wall. Disregarding the damage, the explosion had made, she glanced around, keeping her eyes peeled in the cave for any signs of movement.

"Come out and play, Lucios. Or are you a coward who just hides in the shadows?" Smirking, she was finally beginning to have fun. She felt as if she finally had an advantage in defeating Lucios now that she could see through his hiding in the shadows.

"I am no coward!" Ignoring his comment, she quickly moved out of the way as Lucios attempted to throw Dark Chaos at her.

"You honestly thought that would work?" Zafira mocked him the way he would taunt her. That wasn't going to happen anymore. "Hate to break it to you Lucios, but I have the upper hand now."

After Zafira managed to dodge Dark Chaos, she quickly flew up into the air. While there was still smoke in the air from Lucios' Dark Chaos attack, Zafira hid in the shadow of the cave. Once the smoke cleared, Zafira could see Lucios frantically looking around the cave for her. This caused a smirk to appear on her face.

"Too slow," Zafira whispered in Lucios' ear and kicked him from behind, causing him to slide and hit a wall.

The impact caused Lucios to groan in pain, this caused Zafira to get a smile on her face. She would never admit it out loud, but she liked seeing Lucios in pain. After all, he deserved it for all the cruel things he had done to her and others as well. She ignored Lucios as he glared at her for attacking him.

Zafira threw Lightning Blade, which missed Lucios by a few inches. Taking to the air, she hit him with a Heavenly Destiny, knocking him down once more. Lightning Blade hit Lucios once more, and this time when he stood, he wiped the blood from his mouth. Zafira smirked and threw another Lightning Blade at him and he rolled out of the way, barely escaping. She quickly flew up into the air, becoming almost invisible. She had figured out that when she blocked out distractions from her mind, and she thought about the ability she wanted to use she could increase the power of that skill.

Zafira reappeared behind Lucios and cast Wind Raid at him. Caught off guard, Lucios fell to the floor, but she quickly caught him and swung him to the other side of the cave. Flying towards him, Zafira grabbed Lucios by the neck and tossed him around like a ragdoll. "I'm not done with you yet!"

Zafira's eyes glowed with fire. She was enjoying every minute of this battle. She loved seeing him struggle. He deserved to struggle, after what he did to her family and those other villages. She was going to show him what pain really was. Her rage was not only burning from the loss of her village and her family but from the pain of all the others Lucios had caused pain and suffering. She was going to show him a pain far worse than what he had caused her before it was all said and done.

Her hand then started to glow a bright yellow as it tightened around his throat. Lucios grimaced as she squeezed her burning grip around him harder. Lucios threw Dark Chaos at Zafira, who jumped out of the way. He aimed another shadow at the floor, stirring up dust and giving him the chance to escape. Yet another shadow was conjured from his hand and he used it to blow a hole in the cave wall, which he fled through to retreat.

Darn it! She punched a wall. *He got away!* But then she smirked. No matter. If he thought he could get away, he had another thing coming. It was payback time. Lucios should just admit defeat now; he was going down whether he liked it or not. His demise was near, and it would be easier for both of them if he hadn't run like a coward.

Zafira dashed through the hole Lucios had made, in search of the Blood Demon prince. It seemed as if the hole Lucios had made had led to another part of the cave, from what Zafira could tell. She was surprised that his attack on the interior wall hadn't caused part of the cave to collapse. She kept her guard up though as she traveled through the tunnels, but Zafira knew she was on the right path when she saw blood among the rocks. *I guess he didn't think to clean up some of his wounds before he escaped. The fool.*

It wasn't long before she spotted him up ahead. He didn't appear to be flying though, this only made Zafira smirk. Once she had gotten a little closer to Lucios, but not too close she could see blood running down the side of his body. She couldn't wait to inflict more pain on him. He deserved every ounce. She quietly flew up to Lucios and grabbed him by the back of his shirt. Lifting him into the air, she dropped him to the floor.... hard. She could hear Lucios groan as his body collided with the floor.

Lightning Mayhem.

She then threw a lightning ball at Lucios, and he screamed. His agonizing cry was music to her ears.

"What's wrong, Lucios?" she teased. "Giving up so easily?" Zafira laughed.

"Never!" Lucios recovered and hurled a Dark Chaos at Zafira, who slid out of the way. "Not quick enough," Zafira said, soaring towards Lucios with another Lightning Mayhem.

Lucios coughed as the bolts met with his stomach. It was ironic that a Blood Demon was coughing up blood. *This is the wrath of the Blood Demon Prince? You have got to be kidding me.* He wasn't that tough after all. So much for a challenge. At this rate, saving the world would be easy if Lucios was this weak.

"This isn't over. I'll be back." Groaning, Zafira saw Lucios flap his wings and fly into a different direction from their current location. It appeared to be a struggle for him though, as the side of his body was injured from Zafira's previous assault.

She wouldn't let Lucios out of her sight. Closing her eyes and taking a deep breath, her hand glowed. Most of the time an attack of some kind would appear from her hand, but this was different somehow. The light in the center of her palm floated into the air for a few seconds and then moved so that it was in front of her. It was almost as if the light wanted to be her guide. This confused her, and didn't make any sense, but then again, this whole situation with Lucios, the Blood Demons and her having powers didn't make sense. She would not question it though, she thought she had discovered all her abilities while she was training with Raidon, but she guessed she was wrong.

"Lead me to Lucios," Zafira told the light.

The orb started in a different direction than she had come. He wouldn't get far. She would catch him, and vengeance would finally be hers. It felt like Zafira was running forever, but it was only a few minutes. The light stopped at a dead end. Zafira concentrated and threw a blast at the wall blocking her path.

When the smoke cleared, she looked around and just saw another dark cave. She didn't see Lucios anywhere. Had her powers fooled her? No. That wouldn't happen. Would it? Zafira closed her eyes and concentrated once more. Once she opened her eyes, she started to glow, and her light ability illuminated the entire cave.

"You're not going to get away from me, Lucios." She grinned. "You can try hiding all you want. I will find you."

What seemed like hours, had only been a few minutes. The light leading Zafira to where Lucios was had stopped for a second. She wondered why the light had stopped, but then she saw Lucios flying a few feet away. Her hands then started to glow, *Lightning Flame* she thought, and she threw the conjure toward where she saw Lucios hovering. He was a fool to think he could remain unseen. His time was coming, and that time was now.

Chapter Fifteen: A New Enemy

ZAFIRA WALKED OVER to where Lucios was once the smoke had evaporated. As she got closer, she realized he was no longer amongst the rubble. How is that possible? He couldn't move after a blow like that, she was sure of it.

Zafira let her light energy take over and tossed a sphere of light in a different direction. As the smoke vanished, she saw two people over by Lucios who was in front of her. It was a guy and a female. Who were these people? She had never seen them before. She chucked a light sphere at them, but the man countered the light. Both of their assaults collided, exploding all around them. Zafira glared at the two new figures. Who were they and why were they protecting Lucios? He didn't deserve to be rescued after all the horrible things he had done.

Taking a good look, Zafira saw that the man was tall. He appeared to be five foot eight. The woman next to him however, she appeared to be about five foot five. The man appeared to have black hair that hung past his shoulders with a tint of blue in it and black horns on his head. She couldn't tell what color his real eye color was though, because his eyes were currently red. The guy wore a blue shirt, with grey pants and had a grey cape that went to his knees with blue trimming along the outside. The woman appeared to have blue eyes from what Zafira could tell. They weren't currently red with anger. Her hair was light brown and she had light purple bangs and black horns as well. She wore a lavender dress that went to her ankles, with some slits on the side with some black leggings underneath. The collar of her dress had light blue jewels on it. She had a white cape with light blue trimming on it as well.

"Who are you?" Zafira screamed. "How dare you interfere with my battle!"

She was ready to destroy Lucios, but this man had stopped her. He was a monster just as much as Lucios was. If she had to destroy this man and that lady in order to get to him, she would.

"Fool!" the man said. "Do you know who we are?" Zafira looked at the man who had rage on his face as he asked his question.

"No, should I?" Zafira questioned with confusion filling her face.

"I am King Leveron and this is my wife Queen Marilena. I will not let you destroy my son!" Zafira saw irritation fill this so-called king's face when she didn't know who he and his wife were.

Zafira's eyes widened in shock "Son?"

If they were his parents, where had they been before? Why were they suddenly jumping in?

No matter; she would destroy them all.

"Where were you when I was beating his butt?" Zafira taunted.

"That is none of your concern," King Leveron said protectively. "We saw our son struggling and decided to help." Leveron, moved forward so he was blocking Lucios and Marilena from Zafira's view. Before Marilena's view fully disappeared from Zafira, she saw Marilena console her son.

"Do you know who I am? I am Zafira Rose, the Witch of Elements! Your son will pay for all of the pain he has caused me and others!" Clenching her teeth harder and harder with each word that left her mouth.

Queen Marilena gasped with her body trembling a little. "Leveron, we should escape while we can. Our son needs to recover."

"No!" King Leveron was stubborn. "We will battle!"

"But—"

"Do not question me!"

"I'm sorry, dear," Marilena said with a sigh.

"Relentless Shadow!"

Leveron turned back to focus on Zafira, throwing multiple shadow balls at her. She dodged a few, but she missed one and got hit. The blast was much more powerful then Lucios', but she would not let that stop her. She would defeat these monsters as well. They were no different than their son in her eyes.

Zafira recovered and sprung to her feet, ready to fight. She directed a powerful light beam she called "Sunlight Rush" in the Blood Demon's direction, which caused tremors throughout the cave. She propelled Sunlight Rush once more so they couldn't counter, but King Leveron maneuvered around it with his own shadow beam, "Dark Devastation." Zafira heard Leveron proclaim. The two conjures collided head-on making dust fill the air. Once the dust cleared Zafira saw Leveron standing tall.

Unlike his son, King Leveron stood without a scratch on him. Zafira glared at the Blood Demon family before her and flung Sunlight Rush once again, but it was blocked by King Leveron and he kicked her hard, causing her to slide. He then flung Dark Chaos, but Zafira was able to dodge it. Zafira saw that Leveron was about to throw another strike at her, but when she looked up, the queen was standing in front of her husband.

"You had better be grateful I'm doing this," Queen Marilena said, eyeing Zafira.

Confused as to what she meant, Zafira thought as she stood her ground.

"Dragon Protection," Marilena said.

An abrupt red light erupted in the center of the cave, causing Zafira to shield her face. Once it was gone, the family of Blood Demons was nowhere in sight. Where had they gone? They just vanished? What had this so-called Queen Marilena done? What was that ability of hers? Zafira would probably have to watch out for her the most. She had barely attacked Zafira—unlike her husband—but she had a bad feeling about her.

Zafira took this opportunity to fly back towards the castle. She needed to gather everyone, and they needed to think of a new plan together. This battle was far from over. The true war was just beginning, and she needed a new strategy. Especially since Lucios wasn't her only opponent; now she had to worry about his parents as well. Zafira flew along the few trees as she left the now nearly destroyed cave. If she remembered correctly, she just had to fly straight to head back to the castle.

About an hour later, she appeared in front of the castle where Lucios reigned. The castle that had once stood tall now had a destroyed balcony and crumbling castle walls. The castle gate had a few scratch marks on it and some of the wood appeared to be chipped off, but no major damage. The castle was slowly, but surely being reduced to rubble.

When the castle was within sight, she flew to where she'd last seen Maya. She remembered Lucios keeping her in a room with chains. Zafira soared swiftly towards the dungeon. As Zafira made her way along the castle to the dungeon, she saw walls with holes in them and some of the ceiling was crumbling. Zafira maneuvered her way through some falling stones that were dropping from the ceiling. She could see some demons from Maya's village still fighting with some Blood Demons in the corridors. However, they seemed to be focused on their own battle that they didn't notice Zafira.

Once she had reached the dungeon, she quickly flew in. She saw some injured demons and Maya tending to their wounds, they all had their backs facing away from Zafira. She saw people hanging from the wall with chains around their wrists. Some of the demons had been taken down from their chains, but there were still some demons left who had yet to be unchained. Many of their faces had blood running down the side, as well as stomach or leg wounds.

"Maya!" Worry was leaving Zafira's voice as she said her friend's name.

Zafira saw Maya turn, she had a few scratches on her face and some blood running down her forehead, but she appeared fine. She ran over and hugged Maya. Maya hugged her back and checked on her friend.

"Zafira, you're injured!" Maya said. "Let me help you."

She didn't even know that she was injured. She hadn't felt any pain on her way back to the castle. Then again, all that was on her mind was worry for her friends and the rage that filled her body from Lucios and his parents escaping her grasp. She looked around her body and saw that there was some blood on her right side.

"There's no time," Zafira said. "We have to get everyone out and back to your village—now! We have to rethink our battle strategy."

"Why?" She sounded frightened. "What's happening?"

"We have more than just Lucios to worry about. We must get everyone out of here. Now!"

"Okay," Maya agreed, not questioning her friend anymore.

Maya then started to help Zafira unchaining people. After they had gotten everyone unchained, she gathered everyone together. She looked around the dungeon to make sure that everyone was accounted for. Once she was sure that nobody was missing, she led everyone out of the dungeon. She flew slow, but quick enough to leave the crumbling castle. While she was leading everyone out, she had picked up a few more demons who had survived their battle with the Blood Demons.

Once the group had left the castle entrance, she felt a tap on her shoulder. She looked over to see Maya was pointing to her far right. Zafira looked over and saw Raidon fighting a Blood Demon. His top was slightly torn, and the pants had some tears as well, but he seemed to be okay. Zafira could see various injuries on Raidon, but she knew they would heal quickly having seen it happen before. She remembered when he first started training her and she barely made a scratch on him. The scratches she was able to make with her conjures though, had seemed to heal almost instantly. Watching intensely, Zafira saw Raidon grab the Blood Demon by his wings and fling him into the air. The battle didn't stop there though, from what Zafira could see Raidon's hand was glowing red. Before she could contemplate what was happening, a sword with a black blade and fire with a glow of light surrounding it had appeared in Raidon's hand.

"Flaming Soul Blade." Raidon cried out in anger.

Zafira's eyes widened in surprise as Raidon quickly cut the Blood Demon in half with his sword as if he was nothing. She had never seen such a technique from him before, and seeing it kill a Blood Demon with one strike intrigued her.

"Raidon!" Zafira heard Maya's voice say snapping her out of her thoughts.

Zafira followed Maya and ran towards Raidon. Once they were closer to him, Zafira took in his wounds. Raidon had a few scratches on his face, a leg that appeared to have bite marks on it and his left side had a huge claw wound. She saw Maya, go over to Raidon and start inspecting his wounds, she couldn't help but still feel concerned for her friend.

"Really. I'm fine." Raidon insisted. "You should be more concerned with miss witch girl over there."

Zafira got annoyed with Raidon's comment but decided to let it slide because he was injured. Just because she was a witch didn't mean he had to be rude. Couldn't he show a little bit of emotion for once?

"I'm going to let that slide, but I'd appreciate it if you didn't insult me." Glaring at Raidon with each word that left her mouth.

"Fine. I take it everyone survived the battle?" Raidon questioned wincing as Maya healed the wound in his side.

"Yes. Everyone is alive." Maya answered, finishing up Raidon's wound.

"Very well. That's enough Maya. I do not need my other wounds healed."

"But Raidon—" Zafira heard the concern in Maya's voice, but Raidon just ignored it. She felt for her friend. She just wanted to help.

"There's no need besides it looks like Zafira has something on her mind," Raidon stated. "Isn't that right, Zafira?"

"Yes, but let's head back to the village. It would be safer to discuss the situation there." Zafira specified.

"Very well." Agreed Raidon. "I will levitate everyone back to the castle. Zafira if you wish to fly you may, Maya if you want to run you may do that as well."

Zafira and Maya both nodded in agreement.

Zafira saw Raidon walk over to the demons that had escaped the castle. From the look on his face, she could see that he was impressed that they all managed to survive by the small smile on his face, but it quickly disappeared. Zafira and Maya both walked over to where Raidon was. Once they had joined his side, she decided to address the group.

"Everyone, we have survived this battle, but this isn't the end." Zafira started causing a murmur among the group.

"What do you mean?" Maya asked puzzledly.

"Lucios escaped."

"What do you mean he escaped?" Maya questioned.

"His parents came to save him."

"His parents?"

"That's all I'm going to say for now," Zafira said wanting the conversation to end.

Ignoring her friend, Zafira continued. "For the time being, we will head to the village to recover. I will explain everything once we are all healed and rested up. Raidon is going to be levitating everyone back to the village for a quick retreat. Please give him your full cooperation."

Raidon then put his hands out and closed his eyes. Once he had opened them Zafira could see that they had turned yellow. His hands had started to glow yellow as well. "Solar Protection." Zafira heard Raidon say. The ground started to shake slightly, but not enough to injure anybody. The earth beneath their feet started to split and a massive yellow box appeared with a doorway. Once everyone had entered, the doorway disappeared, and the yellow box lifted into the air and followed Raidon.

It took a lot longer to get back to the village than it did to get to the castle. Zafira was tired, but she couldn't rest, not now. It took two days to get to the village, while the villagers rested in the yellow cube that was soaring them through the trees, Zafira, Raidon, and Maya did not. Their only concern was getting back to the village as quickly as possible. Once they were back at the village, the sun slowly began to rise. Zafira saw Raidon, put his hands out and slowly lower the cube. Once it was firmly on the ground, the once hidden doorway reappeared to let everyone out. Maya and Raidon then tended to the wounded. Luckily, no one had died.

Zafira wandered into the forest, gazing up at the sky.

"Zafira, what is going on?" Maya asked from behind her with Raidon quickly joining them. "Why did we retreat?"

"Lucios isn't our only problem," Zafira said, frantically pacing back and forth.

"What?" Raidon stepped in. "What do you mean? I thought you defeated him."

Zafira turned her attention to Raidon and answered.

"No. I was about to, but then these two figures appeared. They turned out to be his parents and they are much stronger than Lucios. If I am to defeat him, I need to find a way to defeat his parents as well." Zafira was determined, yet overwhelmed. Darn it. This was more frustrating than before.

"What are you going to do then?" Maya asked her.

"I don't know. We need to think of a plan, but right now let's just worry about making sure everyone in the village who fought in the battle recovers." Their safety was of the utmost importance right now.

"Very well," Raidon agreed. "We will think of something when everyone recovers. In the meantime, you should rest as well." That was all Zafira heard him say before he walked away.

"He's right, Zafira. You should rest, and we will think of something when the time is right." Maya said with a slight smile before Zafira saw her follow him.

Zafira couldn't rest—not yet. Lucios and his family needed to die if Zafira had any hope of restoring peace. Dealing with Lucios was one thing, but his parents were far more powerful. Now she had to worry about three powerful Blood Demons instead of one. She had so many thoughts spiraling through her head, but she couldn't worry about them right now. She needed to train to become stronger. Once she was stronger, she would be able to beat Lucios and his family. She could do this; she just had to believe in herself.

Zafira closed her eyes and hit every tree. She tried to attack the trees with multiple attacks of all kinds. She still felt weak though. *How? How could I let Lucios and his family escape? They were right in my grasp and somehow managed to slip through my fingers.* She let out a scream of frustration and punched the earth beneath her feet, causing the ground to rumble. Zafira closed her eyes with tears running down her face and screamed in frustration once more as her wings sprouted from her back. She flew up into the air and threw Eternal Scorch at a tree, but that wasn't enough. *It's not enough! I need something stronger!* Zafira thought. Trying once more, she closed her eyes and put her hand out. *Please give me something new.* Her hand began to glow red; fire slowly left her hand and took the shape of a bow and arrow. Zafira then opened her eyes to see the fiery bow and arrow. It astounded her at first, but she quickly recovered and aimed it at a tree. *Arrow Inferno.* Zafira thought aiming at the tree. Once it hit, the tree burned slightly, but not enough to her liking. She then continued to strike the tree until she was satisfied.

She then moved onto her next element of choice. This time around she worked on light. This seemed to be the element that had the most effect on Lucios. Although, there were some times where the light seemed to have more of an impact than others. Zafira knew how to throw a lightning strike, make a light be her guide, make a light beam, and see through darkness with light and a ball of light but what else could she possibly do? Zafira felt her body begin to glow as she was in the air. She allowed her frustration to fuel her anger and reached her hand to the sky. A beam of light then shot up at the sky, bigger than anything she had done before. This beam felt different in a way, not only did it feel more powerful, but it was a different color....it was a light blue. *Ice Mystic Beam.* It also made her whole-body tingle with a cool yet warm feeling, as she released the conjure. She then summoned the beam once more and struck a tree in a different direction. Continuously, striking tree after tree until, nearly all the trees were destroyed.

Flying down to the ground and landing softly, Zafira then crouched and put her hands on the ground. *Water.* This was her only thought as water began to seep through the ground. Once enough was in her sight, Zafira removed her hand from the ground as the water continued to float in the air. She put her hand out and the water began to move slowly, each time she moved her body the water would as well. As she began to learn to control the water, she started to play around with it a bit. She had made use of her sweat from practicing and added it to her water supply. Once she had enough water, she fired it at a tree with the feeling of a blade. "Hydro Blade," Zafira said after she had cut the tree.

She had also figured out that if she had enough water, she could make a water shield for protection. Zafira felt accomplished with the day's work.

She was going to be ready for the next battle. She was going to win the next time around and bring Lucios and his family to their knees. She would make sure of it. She would make all of them pay dearly.

Chapter Sixteen: Plans & Hunting

THREE DAYS PASSED AND Zafira spent every minute training until her energy had fully recovered. She felt like she was finally ready to face Lucios and his parents. Even though she wanted to go in headfirst and just battle it out, she needed a plan if she and the others hoped to survive. She had to be smart about this situation and think before she acted.

Zafira sat in a hut with Raidon and Maya. She looked over and observed their movements, deep in her thoughts, there had to be some solution that would prevent her friends from getting injured during the next battle. Maya was making sure that Raidon's bandages were fresh on his leg. That seemed to be the only wound left on him, as the other ones had healed already. Maya had seemed to recover as well, her lesions from the battle and the torture she had faced had healed. Zafira wished she could heal that fast, but she knew that was impossible, being human.

"Zafira." Snapping out of her thoughts, Zafira looked up to see that Maya had come to sit next to her.

"Yes? What is it?" Zafira looked at her friend curiously.

"Let me heal your side. If you don't let me heal it, it could become infected."

"Really Maya. It's nothing. I can handle it." Zafira stated with a slight wince. It must have been from the constant training since the wound she had sustained in the battle had healed already.

"No, you can't." Her friend said sternly to Zafira.

Zafira then felt a slight pull on her ear. She looked over to see that Maya had grabbed it and had an annoyed look on her face. Probably from her declining care on her injury.

"I am going to heal it. End of discussion." Zafira could hear the sternness in her friend's voice.

Zafira then took off her top, she didn't care if Raidon was in the room with them because she knew he wouldn't try anything. He was just a friend and her teacher in a way because he helped her with her powers. She saw Maya gather some bandages, some herbs and a paste of some kind judging by what it looked like.

"What's the herbs and paste for?" Her curiosity getting the best of her.

"The herbs are going to help with the healing and the paste will help with the pain."

Zafira then observed Maya as she took the herbs first. She got a small bowl and put the herbs inside of it. She then started to smash the herbs with her fist until they were nothing but a dark green viscous liquid. She watched as Maya applied the pasty liquid to her wound. When it met with her skin Zafira let out a hiss of pain. She saw Maya stop applying the paste made of herbs and nodded at her to continue. Once Maya was done applying the herbs, she applied the other paste, which was white and thick as porridge. This paste gave her body a slight stinging feeling, but it slowly went away and like Maya said it helped with the pain. Lastly, Maya helped Zafira apply the bandages to her wound. She instantly felt better thanks to her friend's medical knowledge.

A small fire shined in the middle of the three friends. Over the fire, a deer cooked that she had accidentally burned, while she was practicing her lightning techniques. At first, she felt bad for the deer that she had hit, but she quickly forgot about it knowing that she needed it in order to survive. Snapping out of that flashback, she watched as Raidon cut up the pieces of deer and handed Maya and herself a piece of the savory meat. As they enjoyed a quiet dinner that evening, everyone wore serious faces. Zafira, Raidon, and Maya were all thinking long and hard about the situation at hand. The three friends couldn't rush into battle like they had last time—Lucios and his family would be expecting that. They needed a different strategy. But what could they do? How could they defeat three vicious monsters instead of one?

"We need to find a way to counter their attacks," Raidon said seriously.

"How?" Maya asked. "Zafira could barely get away from Lucios' parents."

"We'll find a way," Zafira said and concentrated as she ate her dinner. "We just have to put our heads together and think of something."

"Lucios and his family are powerful," Maya said, sounding unsure.

"They may seem powerful, but Lucios seemed tired. I would have destroyed him if it wasn't for his parents interfering," Zafira spat.

Just saying his name made her body engulf in a rage. In Zafira's mind, no Blood Demon deserved to live—especially Lucios and his family. They all deserved to experience a horrible fate that she would be more than happy to deliver.

"MAYBE WE NEED TO FIND a way to separate Lucios from his parents," Raidon said, thinking logically. "I mean if we separate them, then we could possibly defeat them."

"I doubt that we would be able to do that," Maya said with a sigh. "I mean, since Zafira's battle they will probably have their guard up and not let Lucios out of their sight."

"That is probably true, which is why we need to figure out how we are going to separate them from one another," Zafira stated. There just had to be a way.

"What if Raidon and I throw an attack at Lucios' parents," Maya suggested. "It would create an explosion and while they are distracted, Zafira could lift him in the air and carry him away to a secluded area."

"That might work, but we need to have a backup plan, just in case something goes wrong," Raidon said, looking at Maya and Zafira.

"Good idea," Maya agreed with worry in her voice.

"Let's sleep on it and talk more tomorrow," Raidon suggested. "We have time. Besides, Lucios and his family don't know where our village is. Unlike other villages, ours is pretty well secluded."

"Alright." Zafira sighed, hoping Raidon was right. She did not want to see the Blood Demons destroy another village; she didn't think that she could handle any more pain.

As there wasn't much else that they could do at the moment, Raidon, Zafira, and Maya retired for the night. Once their energy was recovered and they got a good night's rest they would think of another plan. Like Raidon said, it was better if they had a backup prepared in case things with their first plan did not go according to plan; she did not want to retreat again. It was better to be prepared than not being prepared and just diving in.

Chapter Seventeen: The Plan of the Great Hunt

ZAFIRA AND HER GANG were near the forest outside of the village. While they thought of a backup strategy, Zafira trained to become stronger. They had to be prepared for anything; there was no telling what the Blood Demons had in store. She knew that whatever they had planned, it wasn't going to be easy to defeat the monsters.

The anger inside of her built at the mere thought of the Blood Demons and Zafira threw lightning at a tree without thinking. Zafira had decided to train some more in the middle of the forest, a few feet away from the village with a small lake. She needed to calm down and use the rational side of her brain if she was to survive. Cutting down a tree with her Lightning Blade conjure, the ground shook as the tree collided with the earth beneath her feet. After the tree had fallen and caused the ground to shake, she turned around to see Maya and Raidon watching her train.

"Zafira, are you alright?" Maya asked, concerned for her friend.

"No! I'm not alright!" Zafira called. "I'm just some witch who's supposed to save the world!"

"Zafira, I know you're going through a lot, but—"

"You have no idea what I'm going through!" she cut off Maya's words. "Were your parents killed right in front of you? Did you lose your entire village?"

No words came out of Maya's mouth. She just lowered her head. "No, but—"

"No, I didn't think so," Zafira cut off Maya's meek reply. "So, don't tell me you know how I feel because you don't!" She threw Lightning Blade once more at a tree.

"Zafira," Maya tried again.

"I'll meet up with you guys later for dinner. I'm going a little deeper into the forest to train." Zafira ran off in the opposite direction of her friends before Maya had the chance to stop her.

She hadn't meant to snap at Maya, but she just needed to be alone. She needed to think and the only way she could do that was by getting away from any distractions and that included her friends. Maya had no idea how she felt, and it was better for her if Zafira put distance between them before her anger made her say something much worse and she regretted it later.

Once she was in a clear spot, she closed her eyes and took a deep breath allowing her mind to clear. She could hear the chirping of birds and the sound of the wind as it rustled through the trees. It soothed the anger that she was feeling. She felt the leaves crinkle beneath her feet and could smell the freshness of the small lake a few feet away from her. Once she was calm, she opened her eyes and shot Lightning Blade quickly at a tree. The tree had burned slightly, but not enough to her liking, so she threw Lightning Blade at it once more. After she attacked the trunk, she threw Heavenly Destiny at it and then swiftly kicked the bark. The trees around her shook, but Zafira didn't care. All she cared about was training to get stronger to defeat her enemies.

When she was done throwing as many blasts as she could, she collapsed. Zafira tried to catch her breath as she stared at the sky, which had darkened since she'd last gazed upwards. Before she got to her feet, she heard a twig snap. Zafira turned her head to see who was there, but only saw a rabbit hopping out of a bush. Zafira sighed in relief and got up. Her body ached from training, but she ignored it; she had to get back to the village. With each step she took Zafira groaned in pain. She had a feeling that Maya was going to be mad at her for overworking herself, but she did not care. She needed to get stronger if she was going to defeat Lucios and his family. She had no time to be weak. Being weak was not an option.

Not too far from where she was, she heard a scream pierce the air. *What was that?* Zafira snapped her head in the direction she'd heard the cry come from. Where had it come from? Was someone in trouble? Should she follow it, or should she head back to the village? She was already out late, judging by the darkened sky, so a few more minutes wouldn't make much difference. She knew her friends would be worried if she stayed out any later than she already was, but she wasn't going to head back now. She was too curious about where the scream had come from. Zafira ran in the direction she heard the scream. As she heard the scream once more Zafira ran faster as adrenaline filled her body.

Through the tree branches, all she saw was carnage. Dead bodies littered the ground. She saw some people were still alive, but they were cowering in fear. She saw families, mothers and children, siblings, and fathers and children shaking with fear. Parents tried comforting their children who cried and siblings who had no parents tried consoling their younger siblings.

A WHOLE BUNCH OF DIFFERENT families were shaking in fear. A lot of them seemed to have sustained some injuries as well. Some had slight cuts, but others had gashes on their sides or their back. Huts were destroyed among a backdrop of burned crops. Blood was everywhere. Zafira didn't know what to do; her body was frozen. It was just like her village all over again.

Zafira couldn't move. She knew it had to be Lucios and his Blood Demons. Who else could have done this? But where was he? She scanned through the trees and didn't see him anywhere, but she knew he had been here.

"Lucios!" Zafira yelled as she came out from the trees and stood before him.

She saw him standing in the middle of the destroyed village just a few feet away with a smirk on his face. Looking around once more at the destroyed village, made Zafira's rage increase tenfold. Her body felt like it was burning from the anger that wanted to be set free. She clenched her fist so tightly that her nails dug into her skin and they started to bleed slightly. She could feel tears building up in her eyes as memories of her dying parents and village clouded her mind, but she blinked them away. Looking at Lucios with angry fire-filled eyes, she wanted nothing more than to end this once and for all. Not only to avenge her family and village's death, but all the other villages that Lucios and his ilk had made suffer.

"Ah, Zafira," he said with a smirk. "So nice to see you."

Zafira wanted nothing more than to wipe that smug smirk off his face. He stood before her with his wings already spread out in his typical black jeans, black cape with jewels, his red shirt, and black boots. She could see blood on his face, making Zafira's eyes widen. She glanced over to where Lucios was standing and saw a lifeless young girl behind his body. He had devoured her like she was nothing. Her eyes widened at imagining his teeth sinking into the girl's neck. However, she quickly recovered refusing to show any kind of fear.

"You will pay for not only devouring that girl, but all the cruel things you have done!"

"Bring it, witch!" Zafira saw Lucios get in a battle-ready position with his fangs bared and his wings arched up in a v formation, ready to pounce at any moment. Zafira looked at Lucios with determination on her face. Whether she stuck to the strategies she and her friends had laid out or not, she was ready to battle. It was time for him to suffer.

Chapter Eighteen: Zafira vs. Lucios

THERE WAS A SILENCE in the wind as Zafira and Lucios stared each other down. The village was silent as the remaining humans ran for cover, peeking from behind the curtains of their huts. Zafira glanced at some of the hiding humans and could feel her fingers twitch with anticipation after seeing the fear in their eyes, but she had to be patient.

Unable to stand still for long, Lucios grew tired and flew into the air. She quickly reacted by sprouting her own wings and following. She threw Lightning Mayhem at Lucios, only for him to easily dodge it. She gritted her teeth in frustration, but threw another; Lucios counterattacked with Dark Chaos, it whizzed past her as if it was nothing. He had used this move so many times on her that it was predictable. Didn't he have any other moves or just the two he was attacking her with constantly?

"Is that all you've got, Lucios?" Zafira couldn't help but laugh. "You are such a weakling!"

"You will pay for that, you good for nothing witch!" Lucios screamed as he soared towards Zafira and threw a bolt of dark energy. His conjure was different from what Zafira could see. It was similar to her lightning abilities but in the form of a shadow.

"Shadow Blade!"

Zafira sighed in mock-boredom, eliciting a narrowed gaze from Lucios. Ever since the battle with Lucios' parents—well, more like his father—Zafira had been training for this moment; getting stronger. It amused her that he had not improved at all.

"Is that the best you can really do?" Zafira smirked, knowing this would get Lucios riled up, and if he was, maybe he would get careless.

"You think that is all I can do?" Zafira saw the rage in Lucios' eyes as she mocked him. A growl of anger escaped from his mouth as Zafira saw Lucios glare at her. She watched as a loud yell of frustration escaped Lucios' mouth.

Her eyes widened as Lucios began to glow—only instead of with light, he appeared to emanate darkness. How was he doing that? Maybe, he was like her in the sense that he had this hidden power inside of him. Maybe he has yet to discover his full powers and they are finally being unleashed. This made Zafira stand her ground, ready to throw her next conjure.

A harsh wind began to pick up, as darkness continued to build and swirl around the Blood Demon. Zafira watched as Lucios built up his energy, the moon and stars that had once filled up the night sky had now disappeared. The sky had become pitch black with a tint of dark purple. The very little vegetation that surrounded the village had now become lifeless. Nothing, but despair seemed to surround the land.

She regained her composure so the shock on her face no longer showed. She wouldn't admit it, but she was glad this hidden power within Lucios had been unleashed. He would be more of a challenge now, but that would make winning even more satisfying. It didn't matter to Zafira whether he had other powers she had not seen before; he was still going to be defeated.

"You wanted to see what I could do? Now you're about to find out!" Lucios yelled with determination in his voice. Zafira looked up at Lucios as she saw his hand glow a dark purple. Energy was building up in his hand.

"Bring it, you Blood Demon!" Zafira was ready to see what this new conjuring of Lucios' was.

"My pleasure, you witch!" Lucios threw a shadow beam at Zafira, which she barely dodged.

"Dark Nova!" Zafira heard Lucios yell in aggravation.

The shadow beam that Lucios released from his hand, appeared to be purple with black electricity surrounding it. Zafira could feel the heat radiating off it as it came closer. Quickly, snapping out of it, Zafira moved out of the way.

Luckily, she recovered and moved out of the way in time. She counterattacked with Lightning Beam and threw multiple shots at Lucios, who escaped a few, but not all. During a pause in the element storm, Zafira spotted Lucios wiping his face. He was sweating, trying to catch his breath.

"That was good, but I'm not out of this battle yet." Lucios flew at Zafira, who ducked under him and threw a fire conjure mixed with light, which she called Phoenix Rising. The light that left her hand was the shape of an orb surrounded by fire. As the orb headed for Lucios, Zafira felt energy built up in her hand and sent small balls of fire towards the moving orb, building up its power.

Putting his arms out protectively in front of his face he blocked the attack. The fiery assault had left a few bleeding scratches and burns on his arms, but nothing major from what Zafira could tell. Once she was close enough, she threw some punches and kicks, all of which he countered. However, it wasn't long before Lucios was caught unaware by a sucker punch. The action seemed to have knocked the rest of Lucios' energy out of him, and he started to plummet to the ground. The energy that was knocked out of Lucios, had returned the night sky to its normal state. The stars and moon once again shined in the night sky. The plants beneath them had recovered what little life they had previously had. Zafira followed his descent with Lightning Flame. She couldn't see whether the attack had done any damage.

Before she could react, she felt a sharp pain in her back and suddenly she too was falling rapidly towards the ground. She quickly shifted her eyes to see that Lucios had quickly recovered and snuck up behind her to attack. She used her wings to steady herself before flying back up into the air, shaking off the ache in her spine. It was nothing; she barely felt any pain now. Zafira held her right hand out, she felt the heat of the light slightly burning her hand, but it didn't bother her. If anything, the heat just made her hand burn a bit, but nothing she couldn't handle. Once the light had built up enough energy, Zafira threw a miniature orb in Lucios' direction.

"Binding Fate!" Zafira exclaimed as she unleashed her power onto Lucios.

She saw him dodge the attack, but a smirk appeared on her face as it continued to follow him. She saw Lucios try to evade it once more, but it just continued to trail behind him. She could tell that he was getting frustrated from not being able to avoid the attack which made a slight chuckle escape her mouth. He was so focused on trying to escape the light orb that as he flew trying to evade it, he accidentally hit his back against a tree and the orb met with his stomach. She could hear him let out a cry of pain as it burned his flesh.

"Come on, Lucios! Giving up already?" Zafira said and throwing Binding Fate once more at Lucios' stomach before he could recover.

Lucios cried out in pain as the blast made contact. It was so loud it echoed throughout the area. She enjoyed seeing Lucios in pain, she was going to end this soon. She had to or Lucios would just end up causing more destruction. She was about to throw another attack at Lucios and end his life, but something quickly struck her from behind causing her to scream in agony and clench her shoulder. She looked around but saw nothing. So, what had struck her? She fell to her knees in pain; she then coughed as she felt a punch to the gut. She looked up to see Lucios, who hit her once more only this time with a shadow ball causing a to scream rip out of her throat.

"Zafira!" She could hear Maya's voice. How had they found her though? They must have either followed her scent or heard her screams.

Zafira heard a familiar voice yell "Flare Blitz!"

She could smell fire as she looked at the ground. Glancing up, Zafira looked to see that Raidon had hit Lucios with a kick surrounded by fire. Zafira climbed to her feet and wiped her face. She winced slightly from the injuries but refused to back down, not when Lucios was so close to being defeated.

"Zafira, you're badly injured. Let me tend to your wounds." Zafira could hear the concern in her friend's voice, but she refused to leave this battle.

"I'm fine," Zafira reassured her.

"Why do you have to be so darn stubborn, Zafira?" She heard Maya shout. "I just want to help!"

Out of the corner of her eye, she saw another blast heading straight towards her friends. Quickly, stepping in front of Maya and Raidon, she managed to block it, but a vast plume of smoke appeared, obscuring her view.

When she could finally see the sky again, Zafira spotted King Leveron and Queen Marilena flying overhead. It seemed to Zafira that they had created a diversion, so that they could help Lucios escape their battle. So, his parents had once again come to save his butt. Zafira rapidly flew into the sky, ignoring her injured shoulder. She quickened her pace, wanting to catch up with Lucios and his family. She saw them landing in a secluded area with nothing but trees and a small stream. She saw them wearing the same royal outfits that they had worn last time, nothing about the parents of Lucios had changed from what she could tell. Zafira saw Marilena, holding her son up who was clenching his stomach in pain.

Looks like I will have to defeat all three of these Blood Demons at once.

"You two!" Zafira said with such distaste in her voice.

"It's so nice to see you again, Zafira." King Leveron said with a smirk.

"Sadly, I can't say the same." Zafira glared at the monsters before her.

"Aw, I think my heart just broke a little." King Leveron pretended to wipe a tear from his cheek.

Zafira only glared at the Blood Demon as he taunted her. He acted like this was a game and it was much more than that. It was a battle of life and death. Zafira thought of all the lives the Blood Demons had destroyed. They had taken happiness away from the world and replaced it with nothing but misery and fear. If she wanted peace, she needed to focus on ending the entire royal line all at once. There was no turning back now.

"You leech! You'll pay for all the things you and your family have done." Clenching her fist and punching a nearby tree in anger. "I swear to it!" Zafira finished as she removed her now bruised hand from the tree.

"We shall see about that, my dear."

Zafira could feel the power inside her building up. Her body heat began to intensify, making Zafira scream. Her insides felt like they were on fire, but she did her best to ignore the pain she was feeling. A fire burned in her eyes as she looked over at the three Blood Demons that prevented her from being happy. Lucios was down, and now it was just his parents. She was ready to face these two.

"Well, are we just going to stand here all day, or are we going to fight?" King Leveron bellowed, growing impatient.

"It would be my pleasure." Zafira grinned before taking to the skies.

As she powered up an attack, Leveron took the opportunity to fly up into the air as well. A shadow ball headed right towards Zafira and she skirted out of the way. They had no time for plans; this battle would decide the fate of their world.

"I hope this ends here." Concern filled Maya's voice, giving it a slight warble.

"I hope you are right, because I have a feeling that a real battle is about to go down. We won't have the others to help this time. It will just be Zafira, Lucios, us, and Lucios' parents." Raidon said letting Maya realize the enormity of the situation at hand and surprising her that he wasn't annoyed with the entire situation.

"You're right, but we still have to be prepared for anything," Maya said as she ran ahead. She wanted to reach Zafira and Lucios as soon as possible. The sooner they reached Zafira the sooner they could help her out.

"You're right. Be on your guard." Raidon said as he and Maya both picked up their pace.

Once they got to the clearing both Raidon and Maya stood their ground. They looked through the trees slightly and saw Zafira and Lucios. They were shocked at what they saw just like Zafira had been. There was blood and dead bodies everywhere. Had Lucios caused this? Maya and Raidon were both more determined than ever to help Zafira defeat this monster. *How could someone be so heartless?* Maya thought.

"Keep your guard up. If Lucios can cause this much damage to a village, who knows what else he can do. We can't underestimate him." Raidon said to Maya snapping her out of her thoughts.

Maya nodded as she looked at Raidon as he spoke. They both came out from the trees and ran in the direction of their friend only to be hit and go flying in different directions from the force of the blast. Maya and Raidon both got up slowly and looked at each other. What was that? Where had it come from? Maya and Raidon both held their ground looking in every direction. They saw nothing though. What was that?

Just then another blast was heading straight towards Maya, but she didn't see it coming. Luckily, Zafira had seen it and didn't care if Lucios was alive or not. She was more concerned with her friend's safety rather than her own, she blocked the attack with her arms and body which caused her to go flying. Her back slammed into a tree and she groaned in pain from the impact.

"Zafira!" Maya worriedly exclaimed.

Zafira got up from the hit as if it was nothing and wiped the dirt off her face. She took a deep breath and glanced around. She didn't see anything, so where was the blast coming from? It couldn't have been Lucios right? There was just no way seeing as Zafira had hit him hard.

"I'm fine," Zafira reassured Maya trying to figure out where the blast had come from.

Lucios glanced out of the corner of his eye at his parents. They couldn't see him, but he could see them. He would attack when the moment was right, but for now, he would let them enjoy their fun. He knew his father and he

WANTED TO HAVE SOME fun with this witch. He would lay low for now and would attack when the time was just right.

"Well, shall we continue to see who will decide the fate of the world?!" King Leveron said growing impatient.

"It will be you whose fate has already been decided. Die you Blood Demon!" Zafira said and flew up into the air at rapid speed and powered up a blast.

As the blast was powering up, Leveron took the opportunity to fly up into the air as well. Leveron's Dark Chaos headed right towards Zafira and she flew out of the way and threw her first blast right at Leveron. And so, the battle had begun.

Chapter Nineteen: Fated Destiny

ZAFIRA HAD STARTED by throwing Heavenly Destiny at King Leveron and Queen Marilena while Maya and Raidon arrived on the scene. Leveron threw a Shadow Disc at Zafira, but it was obvious he was frustrated at the interference of Zafira's friends.

She saw Raidon take the opportunity to build up some fire in his hand and threw a Fire Fist at the king, but he easily dodged it and countered with throwing his move Night Destruction. Zafira saw Raidon build up some fire in his hand and once he had enough energy, he released the fire that took the form of a dragon.

"Dragon Bite!" Raidon proclaimed.

Taking the opportunity of Raidon's attack distracting Leveron, she held both of her hands out, and her hands started to a glow a burnt umber. She felt the heat burning her hand slightly, as a swirl of fire headed towards Leveron as well hoping that one of the two attacks would hit him, but of course, it was blocked by Marilena. She counteracted with a barrier and once the barrier had cleared, she threw the move Relentless Shadow in Zafira's direction.

She flew in the sky, dodging each of Marilena's Shadow Hives which were little balls of shadow with a dragon head that could poison the victim if bitten. Recovering and looking for an open spot, she put both her hands out and closed her eyes, taking a deep breath and erasing all thoughts from her mind. She reopened her eyes and threw two beams of light that appeared to be light yellow from each hand in Leveron and Marilena's direction. The two beams of light had left her hands feeling slightly heated, but it wasn't anything she couldn't handle. She didn't see how they would be able to block this attack.

The beam of light hit them dead on, the impact causing the ground and surrounding trees to shake. Marilena and Leveron were up in the air as soon as they'd recovered, and Zafira was furious the attack didn't even faze them. No matter. They would be destroyed one way or another. She wasn't planning on giving up any time soon.

Leveron looked at his wife, who nodded as if quietly speaking to one another as to which technique to use next. Marilena raised her hands and then some blobs started to form in her hands. They appeared to be red and spongy looking. Zafira's eyes widened with curiosity. How could these blobs be a threat? She had never seen this technique, but she kept her guard up, nonetheless. Zafira flew up higher and was ready for an assault, but it didn't come. Marilena pointed her hands toward the ground where Zafira's friends were, and Zafira attempted to fly down to protect them, but Leveron threw Dark Chaos at her full force. That shadow ball had thrown Zafira back a few feet in the air, but she did a flip and recovered.

Once Zafira had recovered, she looked down to where Marilena had aimed her spell and came to realize it wasn't an attack. There were now Blood Demons battling Raidon and Maya. *But how was that possible? All the Blood Demons were in the surrounding villages and the castle, so how were they here?* These Blood Demons looked different from the usual ones she had seen, though. They didn't appear to look like actual Blood Demons. They didn't have human eye color or hair. They didn't have pale skin; in fact, they didn't have any human characteristics. Their entire body was red, red eyes, red skin, even their fangs were red. It was like they were made from actual blood itself.

Zafira snapped out of her thoughts and focused on Marilena, who had a smirk on her face. "You seem to be in shock," the queen said. "What's the matter?"

"What did you do?" Curiosity and rage filling her mind as she watched Raidon and Maya battle these new Blood Demons.

"You see, my dear Zafira, I am one of the few Blood Demons that have the ability to create other Blood Demons, thanks to a spell called Dragon's Gift," Marilena said, a full grin stretching her lips. "It is such a gift, isn't it?"

"Isn't she wonderful?" Leveron said, wrapping his arms around his wife and kissing her roughly.

Zafira looked at the couple with disgust. This was no time to be mocking her or having a make-out session.

Getting tired of seeing Marilena and Lucios make out in front of her, Zafira built up light in her hands. She waited until there was enough energy in her hand. She then released a disc of light in the shape of a crescent moon surrounded by fire and hurled it at the couple standing in front of her.

Moonlight Rage. Zafira thought, not wanting to announce her attack and let Marilena and Leveron get away.

Marilena and Leveron managed to break apart and move out of the way in time, glancing at each other and then back at Zafira. The lovers each put a hand out and aimed at her. Their hands begin to glow black, two balls of dark energy built up in their hand, from what Zafira could see. Once a small shadow each left their hand, the shadows combined with each other to form one enormous shadow ball with purple electricity surrounding it. The ball of shadow and electricity headed for Zafira, but before the dark attack headed towards her it quickly switched directions catching her off guard. She looked to see that ball of darkness and electricity was heading right for Maya and Raidon. She flew in the direction of her friends, but she was stopped by a kick to the gut. The wind was knocked out of her and she glanced up to see that Leveron had delivered the blow. He had a few scratches on his face and his shirt was a little torn, but there were barely any injuries on him.

"We're your opponents, not the Blood Demons. Pay attention and fight!" King Leveron said and kicked Zafira savagely once more, as blood began to trickle out of her mouth.

Zafira fell hard and slammed her back against the ground. She groaned in pain and slowly got up. The height of the drop had caused pain to ricochet throughout her body, but surprisingly nothing was broken. She didn't have time to think about the pain. All she cared about was the safety of her friends. She wished they would have never joined this battle. This was her fight, not theirs. *Maya. Raidon. I'm going to win this battle for you.*

She decided to sprint towards her friends, but before she could get close, a wall of shadow blocked her path. She tried to run through the wall of shadow, but it sent an electric shock through her body and flung her back. Zafira quickly pushed herself up and stood her ground. Zafira looked up and saw that the wall had prevented her from reaching her friends. She clenched her teeth in anger. This was getting annoying.

"Like we said," the queen called, "We're your opponents, not the Blood Demons!" She threw a Shadow Disc at Zafira which she blocked with her arms.

Zafira looked at Marilena and Leveron, then both of her friends. This battle was going to be a lot harder than she expected. Zafira closed her eyes and put her hands out. She mustered up as much firepower as she could and threw a ball of fire mixed with pulses of electricity at the king and queen. She felt her hand glow red as a bow and arrow made of fire appeared in her hand, she shot Arrow Inferno at the wall of shadows that Marilena and Leveron had built. Her arrow managed to make a small circle in the wall which she quickly flew threw to get to her friends.

AGAIN, SHE WAS HALTED with another advance, a ball of darkness shooting her out of the sky. Zafira landed safely on the ground but glared at the Blood Demons Marilena had created looking down upon her. *Darn it!* Zafira felt her hand slightly tingle and glow yellow as a ball of light formed. She flew up swiftly so that she was face to face with the Blood Demon who interfered with her attempt to save her friends. She swiftly thrust the ball in the Blood Demon's stomach before he had the chance to attack her.

This fight seemed never-ending, but it had only been a few minutes. *Hang in there, Maya and Raidon. I'll get to you two as soon as I can. Just try and hold out a little longer.* She then felt a sting to her back. She turned to see that Leveron and Marilena had once again joined her. She felt her hand glow red once more and released a beam of fire called Fire Bolt in their direction. The earth around her shook a little from the impact of it hitting the trees slightly.

Once she had thrown the attack, Zafira flew until she was far enough away from the action and hid in a tree. She leaned back against the tree to catch her breath. The battle had barely started, but Leveron and Marilena combined were tougher than Lucios. If she didn't figure out a way to defeat them, her world was doomed. No. She couldn't think like that. Zafira closed her eyes to rest and tried to gather her thoughts.

Chapter Twenty: Flashbacks of the Past

THE BATTLE WITH LUCIOS' parents was taking its toll on Zafira. As much as she hated to admit it, they were stronger than her. How could she beat two Blood Demons who had more power than she and her friends? She hoped Raidon and Maya were okay. It was as if right at that moment Maya had read her thoughts; Zafira heard a whisper in the wind that sounded exactly like her friend's voice.

I hope you're okay Zafira. We know you didn't abandon us. I know you'll find us.

She sighed in relief as soon as she got the message. Zafira felt her confidence increase with the knowledge of knowing that her friends were safe. She knew she had to think of a plan, but right now she needed some rest so she could regain her strength.

As soon as she closed her eyes, she dreamed of a simpler time; when her parents were alive; back when she was happy. When there were no Blood Demons in control, and everyone was free.

She ran around her village with a huge smile plastered on her face. Everything was peaceful in her village; there were no Blood Demons. She giggled as she looked at her parents and waved with a grin. Her mother Sophina had beautiful jet-black hair, and eyes as blue as the sky. She had a pale complexion, but she wasn't too pale. Her father Ryker, on the other hand had dark brown hair, that was short at the time and had bangs that slightly covered his green eyes. He had a slim but muscular physique as well, compared to her mother who was small and dainty. Zafira had light brown hair that went a little past her shoulders and blue eyes. She wore a light green dress with some roses embroidered on the sleeves that her mother had designed for her because her parents were attending a festival that her village held every year called The Owl Festival. The Festival consisted of different owl lanterns, food booths with various owl names, there were performers dancing the owl dance in costumes and there were even a few different activities for kids, such as making owl masks and dancing to music. Another flashback then filled her mind, she and her parents were walking around the village stopping by the different huts. Her mother was a healer in her village and always tended to sick people. Her father was the village leader and always made sure that everyone was treated equally. He had a reputation for being stern but fair, when it came to running the village. Zafira watched as her mother healed the last person of the day which was an elderly lady. She had snow-white hair and green eyes, her smile surrounded by wrinkles and she wore a brown dress with a white apron. "Thank you." Zafira heard the elderly lady say to her mother. "No trouble, Ryker and I just want to make sure that everyone in our village is cared for." Zafira heard her mother say. "Bless you." The lady said and slowly fell asleep on the mat of her hut. "Zafira, whatever you do when you are older, always be kind," Sophina said to her daughter. "Okay, but what if the person is mean to me?" Zafira asked with her curious little mind pondering over her mother's words. "Still be kind. Kindness is more powerful than you know." Her father Ryker said. "Okay. If you say so, Daddy." Zafira smiled back at her mother and father and grabbed each one of their hands in hers. Then the once happy memory turned into one of despair. Zafira was older now at the age of fifteen. The previously bright village that she knew no longer existed. Darkness, fire, and screams replaced the light. The once bright sky had turned dark and fires burned all around her village. The huts were burned down and all she heard were the cries of her fellow villagers as the Blood Demons sunk their teeth into them. Blood Demons swarmed from every corner of the village, destroying everything in their path. Including her parents. From what she could see the Blood Demons had the wings of a dragon. They also had fangs that devoured the humans in her village including her parents. Zafira remembered freezing as blood-red eyes looked at her. She remembered her body not being able to move, completely frozen in terror at the scene unfolding around her. Once the Blood Demon stepped on a twig, it snapped her out of her thoughts, and she ran away from her once-happy village.

Zafira awoke with a scream, sweat running down her face. Wiping her forehead, she slumped against the tree. The Blood Demons had probably heard her, but after a quick glance around, she saw no immediate threat. She tried to think of her next move, but nothing came to mind. She had attempted to throw electricity, fire, earth, and water, but to no avail... nothing worked. Zafira wished her parents were there, they would have known what to do. *Mother, Father, I need you and your guidance. Please help me and tell me what I should do?* She glanced around the corner of the tree, but she didn't see Leveron or Marilena. She was safe for the time being. She closed her eyes and thought of her parents.

Zafira then opened her eyes and saw the mark on her wrist was beginning to glow. It glowed so bright that it nearly blinded her. A bright light then left her mark. She looked to see the light turn into two figures, who just happened to be her parents. It was as if the mark on her wrist knew she needed their guidance and had summoned them just for her.

Zafira.

It was really her mother's voice. Her eyes slid slowly closed and then quickly reopened them just to make sure this was reality and not another dream. This had only happened a few times and it was still hard to believe that her parents were there before her. Zafira could feel tears welling in her eyes; she wanted to hug them, but she knew she couldn't. All she could do was plaster on a smile as she looked to them for guidance, they needed to know she was okay now more than ever. Her parents each had a glow to their body like the last time. Her father's hair was still long, and chocolate brown and he still had green eyes. Her mother still had her beautiful blue eyes and her jet-black hair that was as dark as the night sky. Nothing had changed from the last time that she had seen them. They were the same as before.

"Mother, Father, what do I do?" she asked. "I have tried everything I can think of to defeat Lucios, but now I have his parents to worry about as well. What do I do?" she cried, the tears finally rolling down her cheeks. "I'm losing hope and I don't know exactly which way to turn anymore."

"Zafira, my dear," said her mother. "There is no need to cry. You can do this. If you continue to doubt yourself, you will never succeed. I know it's hard to hear, but it's true." Zafira could hear the concern in her mother's voice as she tried to comfort her.

"Your mother is right," her father agreed. "If you don't believe in yourself, there is no way you will defeat them." His usual stern countenance becoming soft and sincere as he gazed upon his daughter.

"But no matter what I do or what attack I throw at them, they just don't seem to stay down. King Leveron and Queen Marilena are nothing like their son. Lucios is much easier to fight than those two—he'd already be defeated if his parents hadn't stepped in."

"We know that you are frustrated," her mother said, "you have to rid yourself of frustration and not let your emotions get the best of you. Your elemental powers are the key to defeating Lucios and his family. You must tap into yourself and harness the power you have deep inside. You have barely honed your powers. You must look down deep within and your true power will come out."

"But how do I do that?" Zafira protested. "I have tried to do that numerous times, but nothing changes. And why didn't you ever tell me that I had powers in the first place!" She hit a tree, making its branches tremble, finally giving a voice to her frustrations.

"We are sorry that we kept this from you, dear," her mother replied. "We had hoped we would be able to tell you when you were a little older, but you truly are special, Zafira. Not many humans are born with such gifts." She saw her mother tear up from having not had the opportunity to be the one to tell her about her powers. She wished she could wipe the tears from her mother's eyes, but she knew that was impossible.

"I wish I could remain calm," Zafira sighed, "but when I think about what those Blood Demons have done, I get so angry. They not only killed you and destroyed our entire village, but they have murdered others as well. They have also made humans and demons into their slaves and when they are finished with them, they suck the blood right out of them and leave them to rot." Another burst of tears stung her eyes.

"Oh, that's terrible," her mother whispered. "I wish your father and I could help more, but you have to defeat them on your own."

"Farewell, my dear daughter," her father said before she could respond. Already, her parents were fading before her. "I love you."

"No, please don't go! Don't leave yet!" But it was too late; they were gone.

Every time Zafira saw her parents it hurt more and more; each time they vanished was like losing them all over again. She wished they were still alive and never went away. Overwhelmed with a wave of grief, she thought of all the demons and humans who had lost their lives because of those Blood Demons. Zafira let out a frustrated scream.

THERE WAS NO TIME FOR tears and crying; she dried her face. She had to be strong and listen to what her parents had said. She had to believe in herself and not lose control, which was something she already knew. She closed her eyes and took a few deep breaths trying to center her thoughts. Once she was calm enough, she opened her eyes and started to think. *What could be their weakness? There had to be something.*

Zafira recalled a previous meeting with her parents; remembering that they said that anything with light seemed to have an impact on Blood Demons. He seemed to be greatly affected by it, but whenever she threw a light technique at him, it barely phased him. So, what was she doing wrong? Was she throwing the wrong conjure or was she just not powerful enough?

Leveron and Marilena had to be weak against light as well. However, she had used that element and never hit them with it. They both appeared faster and stronger than their son. Maybe if she increased the power, and she funneled into it she would be able to defeat them. She didn't know if it would work, but she would give it a try.

Just then, the trees shook as a Shadow Disc was thrown at Zafira. She took cover behind another trunk and looked over to see Leveron and Marilena standing before her with smirks on their faces.

The battle was going to continue and thinking of a plan was now out of the question. Zafira just hoped that Maya and Raidon were handling themselves well, seeing as she had her hands full with these two. Sprouting her owl wings as she hid behind the trunk, Zafira held out her hand and powered up her Arrow Inferno conjure. Ready to strike at the right moment.

Chapter Twenty-One: The Fate of the World

SHE NEEDED TO END THE battle before everything in her world got worse than it already was. Their smug expressions only made her angrier—it was as if they were quietly mocking her; daring her to make a move. Well, if it was a move they wanted, that was what they were going to get.

In a twirling motion, Zafira launched into the sky and pulled her Fire Arrow back and released it at the Blood Demons below. They split up before expanding their dark wings, a dangerous look in their eyes as they took to the air as well. She quickly spun around until she was facing both the Blood Demons who were in separate directions. Putting an arm out in each direction of the royal Blood Demons, Zafira felt the heat of her hands intensify. Ignoring the burning sensation in her hands, she released a beam of lightning mixed with fire in both Marilena and Leveron's direction. The impact of the beams had caused an explosion and some trees to shake. Hoping that the beams had hit both the royal Blood Demons, Zafira waited until the glare that was still refracting through the trees from the bright explosion died down. The hope that she had on her face disappeared when she saw Marilena and Leveron unharmed.

"Well," Zafira said impatiently, "are you two monsters just going to float in the air all day?"

"Just remember you asked for it." King Leveron flew at Zafira in a burst of movement. Once Leveron was close enough, Zafira saw that he was ready to throw a Shadow Disc at her.

Zafira easily saw the Shadow Disc approaching and bolted out of the way, but Marilena countered—she dodged another Shadow Disc from being thrown at her as well. Zafira let light build up in her hands and threw a light beam mixed with electricity and fire called Fiery Current. The beams soared through the sky at an incredibly high rate of speed and the brightness of the beam was blinding. The force was so bright and powerful that Leveron and Marilena shielded their eyes. While they were busy, Zafira flew higher into the sky. Once she was high enough, she raised her hands and threw a powerful Heavenly Destiny in the direction of Leveron and Marilena. Being so focused on Lucios' parents Zafira didn't notice Lucios sneaking up on her.

Lucios snuck up behind her and threw a Shadow Ball that was more powerful than any she had experienced. Hitting her from behind, Zafira cried out. *How could I be so careless? I completely forgot that Lucios was here, even if he was injured. I shouldn't have let my guard down.*

Suddenly, she was freefalling, but Zafira brushed it off before she could hit the ground. Once she was in the air once more, Zafira spotted the younger Blood Demon and saw that his parents had recovered. *Darn it!*

"Nice of you to join us, Lucios." She glared at him. "Are you ready to face defeat with your parents?"

"It is you, my dear Zafira, who is about to face defeat." Getting a good look at him, Zafira saw that he was indeed still injured from their previous battle. He hadn't fully recovered which meant that he was not at full strength. She could still see the cuts on his body and heard the pain behind his voice as he spoke.

She laughed as if Lucios had just told her a joke. This only angered the Blood Demon more. Zafira didn't know how a Blood Demon who seemed to be in pain from their previous battle was going to be able to defeat her. The thought amused her greatly.

"Is this a joke to you?" he bellowed. "Do I amuse you?"

"As a matter of fact, you do." She couldn't help but giggle. "If you think a weakling like you can beat me, you have another thing coming."

Before Zafira could react, Lucios was slamming her against a tree with his hand around her throat. She could see the red in Lucios' eyes intensify from his anger. The anger she felt inside only burned brighter. His grip became tighter and tighter, nearly causing her to lose consciousness. Zafira wrapped her fingers around Lucios' wrists to pry him off her, but he didn't budge. She refused to let him have the satisfaction of defeating her. Losing was not an option. Lucios was so preoccupied in choking her to death that he did not notice the attack that was heading straight towards him.

"Tell me, who's the weak one now?" Lucios said with a sinister laugh.

"You," Zafira choked out which made his expression quickly shift into one of confusion.

"What are you—"

"AH!" Lucios yelled in agony as a blast from behind hit him, causing his grip to loosen and for Zafira to fall to the ground. The swirling fire beam had hit Lucios directly on the back, Zafira watched from her spot on the ground as Lucios plummeted down to the earth.

Once Zafira was on her knees, she slowly tried to catch her breath. When she was no longer panting, she squinted into the sky to see not only Lucios' parents hovering in the air fully recovered, but also Maya and Raidon standing on a tree branch. Maya had a concerned scowl, but Raidon appeared determined. They both jumped down from the tree and landed by Zafira's side.

"Nice of you guys to finally join us," Zafira said sarcastically as she got to her feet.

"Well, sorry," Raidon said, matching her tone. "We were a little preoccupied."

"Just get ready to fight." Zafira was ready to end this battle once and for all.

"Why do you think we're here?" Raidon slightly raised his voice.

"Okay. Enough you, two," Maya chimed in. "We should be fighting Lucios and his family, not each other." She stepped between Raidon and Zafira.

Focusing on the situation at hand, they got into offensive positions and braced themselves. Zafira flew into the air and Maya and Raidon struck from below. Zafira flew at Lucios, and Raidon and Maya combined a wind and fire beam called Whirlwind Flare and flung it towards Lucios' parents. Each of them now had their own enemy to face.

Zafira put her hands out and let the energy inside of her build up. She felt her hands heat up slightly then chill. Lightning, fire and ice combined into one beam and headed towards Lucios as he tried to reach his parents. Once the beam had met with his body a howling cry left his mouth. Zafira saw his body begin to fall to the earth. Quickly racing to catch him before he could fall, she grabbed him from behind and started to glow. She started thinking back to what her parents had meant. Light was the key to Lucios' defeat. She had found it. The light was inside of her and she just had to learn how to unleash it which had finally happened. By putting aside all her thoughts and harnessing her power, Zafira had unleashed her full power. Lucios screamed as the light surrounding Zafira contacted his skin, burning him. She considered it payback for the first time they met. He deserved all the pain she inflicted upon him. He didn't deserve any kind of mercy. His screams were a sweet symphony to her ears as the light seemed to burn his skin, slightly burning Zafira as well, but she could take the pain.

"Lucios!" Marilena cried for her son.

The queen was about to fly towards Lucios as her motherly instincts took over, but she was stopped by a blast of wind throwing her in the opposite direction of her son. Marilena tried to fly in every direction to get to her son, but Maya continuously slung wind attacks at her. Maya took the opportunity to throw a tornado made of wind that picked up trees and leaves along the way, knocking her into a tree.

"You're my opponent, not Zafira's!" Maya yelled as she threw a tornado made of wind which she named Hurling Wind at the queen. "So why don't you focus on battling me?"

"Marilena!" Leveron called out.

Lucios' mother brushed herself off as she stood and flew back into the air. She nodded at her husband as if she was reassuring him that she was okay, and Leveron faced back towards his own fight with Raidon.

Maya threw a Wind Kick at Marilena and she threw a Shadow Disc right back. Both collided, causing them to slide back. Maya threw a Wind Punch and Marilena threw a Shadow Ball. They each threw punch after punch, kick after kick, but they were getting nowhere. Each attack seemed to be futile.

Zafira wanted to help her friends out, but she had her own hands full with Lucios. This battle could be over once and for all with his demise. Lost in her thoughts, Zafira didn't realize that Lucios had left her grip.

Lucios threw a Shadow Ball at Zafira, who escaped her thoughts just in time to dodge the attack. She retaliated with Lightning Flame, which Lucios flung away like it was absolutely nothing. She flew into the air and closed her eyes. She began to glow brightly as she gathered as much light energy as she could. She started gathering light from the moon; both her village's moon and the Blood Demon's moon. As she absorbed both moons energy, she felt her power increasing tenfold. Once she opened her eyes a powerful beam of light shined in multiple directions, stopping the current battles at hand. She looked at Maya, Raidon, and Lucios and his parents as they stared at her in awe.

Holding her hands out in front of her, Zafira concentrated as the energy she was holding built up. Once she was at full power, she spotted Lucios and glared.

"No longer will you torture anybody else; no longer will people live in fear!" Zafira glared down at Lucios with such a hatred that if you looked her in the eye, your skin would crawl.

She put her hands out above the sky. The sky started to get darker and thunder and lightning made its way to the once clear sky. Zafira waited for the lightning to make its way towards her. Once it was within her reach, she threw the powerful bolt of lightning at him before he had the chance to move away.

Zafira saw Lucios' body beginning to burn from the lightning striking his body. The screams that left his mouth made the smile on Zafira's face appear bigger. Zafira glanced down as the lightning continued to electrify Lucios and saw his parents and her friends frozen in place from what was happening to him.

"Lucios!" Marilena cried, but it was too late. Her son would be gone before she had the chance to reach him.

"Now to finish you off!" Zafira said, ready to deliver one final attack at the monster known as Lucios. She wanted to make sure that he was dead for good. The sky crackled as Zafira gathered lightning in her hand. Once it was in her hand Zafira combined light to the lightning which made it glow a bright yellow instead of an icy-blue-white.

"No!" Marilena cried and started to head towards her son, but Maya threw Tornado Blitz that knocked her to the ground.

"Zafira! Finish him off! Now!" Maya yelled.

"Brilliant Andromeda!" Zafira proclaimed as she threw the lightning mixed with light conjure at Lucios, who screamed in pain louder than he had from any previous assault. The smoke from the blast cleared and Lucios was nowhere in sight. She flew to where he had been previously sprawled in pain. His face was partially burned, and his legs and arms were burned as well. The attack on Lucios was so powerful that she saw Leveron was unable to move and Marilena was the only one left unharmed. Zafira saw that Marilena did not even have so much as a scratch on her body meaning she must have evaded the attack with her shield or took cover in the trees somehow. However, from what she could tell, half of Leveron's face was burned and his whole torso was burned along with his arms and legs. There was no way he was going to survive when so much damage had been done to his body as well. The smile on Zafira's face grew; she was ready to destroy the last royal Blood Demon.

However, before she had the chance, Zafira saw Marilena clap her hands together and a puff of smoke appeared around her. Zafira ran at the smoke that appeared, but when she ran through it nothing was there. It was as if Marilena had just completely vanished. Not a single trace was left of her.

"Darn it! She escaped!" Maya was annoyed.

"It's all right," Raidon said. "Lucios is dead, as well as his father, Zafira just had to kill him."

"But what if Marilena tries to get revenge for her son and husband's deaths?" Maya asked with worry.

"Then we'll be ready," Zafira answered, joining them. "But for now, all we should worry about is restoring peace."

"You're right." Maya, abandoning her negative theories.

"In the meantime, let's restore what the Blood Demons have destroyed," Zafira said as she looked at the damage from the battle. It was sinking in, it was over...for now.

"Let's get to work," Raidon said.

Zafira then soared to where Lucios' unmoving, burned body lay. Once she was close enough, she reached out with one hand. As she concentrated, light filled her palm and she released Heavenly Destiny. He let out one more painful cry before he disintegrated into nothing but ash.

Zafira, Maya, and Raidon then headed to each village that the Blood Demons had destroyed. Each village Zafira stopped at, she helped the villagers by replanting their food supply, Raidon helped rebuild destroyed huts, and Maya tended to the wounded. If there was something to be done, then they did it. They even gave proper burials to the dead. They dug graves and put up tombstones for those that had passed. Once everything was back to normal, Zafira became the guardian of the villages. This meant that she would watch over every village to make sure that they were safe and well taken care of. Once every village was tended to, which took nearly a week, her wrist began to glow. This surprised her still, as she was still not used to it. The light that had once led her to Lucios started leading her towards the middle of the forest. Once she was there, she saw nothing at first, but heard "Zafira."

Zafira turned around to see the silhouettes of her parents. She wished they were still alive to share in her victory against the Blood Demons, well for

Leveron and Lucios. She knew Marilena would surely be back for revenge in due time.

"Mother, Father" Zafira started. "I did it. I defeated Lucios and Leveron."

"We know my dear, and your mother and I couldn't be prouder." Zafira's smile grew as she saw the smile appear on her father's face.

"But I let Marilena get away." Zafira's smile disappeared as she mentioned the Blood Demon queen's name.

"That is alright," Sophina reassured Zafira.

"YOUR MOTHER AND I BOTH know that when the time comes to face Marilena, you will be ready." Zafira's smile once again made its way to her face as her parents reassured her she had done her job.

"We have watched you restore peace to the villages; you can also bring life back to the earth. All you have to do, my dear daughter, is combine three simple powers, earth, light, and water," Ryker explained.

"Is that really true?" Zafira questioned.

"Yes, my dear."

"Your father and I love you, Zafira," her mother stated. "And we will always be with you."

"Take care Zafira. I love you." Zafira's father said.

Her parents slowly disappeared. Once they were gone, Zafira closed her eyes and felt the familiar pain of her wings ripping through her back. She then flew up into the air. She reopened her eyes and put her hands out raising them towards the sky. The once-clear sky was now covered in gray clouds, and rain had started to fall. She flew to the ground and put her hands out before her until they were glowing bright yellow. She then slammed them on the ground and the destroyed earth started to rejuvenate with life. She saw flowers, trees, and plants slowly return to life. Once everything in the area had come back to life, Zafira flew high and began to soar through the region, to watch the combination of her light, earth, and water powers work. Zafira then flew back to her new home, her friend Maya's village with a proud smile on her face.

While she flew back to the village, thoughts clouded her mind. She could face any challenge that came her way. Even if that meant that one day, she would have to face one final battle with Marilena, who would surely want to avenge her husband and son. Zafira was prepared for the future. She had become stronger and wasn't afraid to face whatever Marilena threw at her. She would be ready.

Don't miss out!

Visit the website below and you can sign up to receive emails whenever Courtney Kirkpatrick publishes a new book. There's no charge and no obligation.

https://books2read.com/r/B-A-LWMI-CYTAB

BOOKS 2 READ

Connecting independent readers to independent writers.

About the Author

Courtney Kirkpatrick writes fantasy. She discovered a passion for it when she won her first poetry contest in high school. Her poem "Sarah," was published in the book *Stars in Our Hearts Insight*. Hailing from New Jersey she endured bullying, hydrocephalus, and even a learning disability. Her mission is to inspire her readers through fantastical plots and magical yet relatable protagonists.

courtneyannkirkpatrick@gmail.com

https://www.facebook.com/OfficialCourtneyKirkpatrick/

Made in the
USA
Monee, IL